# THE SECRET POLICEMAN

When a superintendent in the Security Branch is murdered, top detective Jack Forrester is assigned to the case. Realising his new colleagues are keeping vital information from him, Jack Forrester sets out to catch the killer on his own. But Forrester soon becomes ensnared in a web of drug traffickers, Moslem vigilantes, and international terrorists. As he delves deeper into the superintendent's past, he realises he must make an arrest quickly — before he becomes the next police casualty . . .

*Books by Rafe McGregor*
*in the Linford Mystery Library:*

THE SECRET SERVICE

RAFE McGREGOR

---◆---

# THE SECRET
# POLICEMAN

*Complete and Unabridged*

**LINFORD**
*Leicester*

First published in Great Britain

First Linford Edition
published 2008

British Library CIP Data

McGregor, Rafe
    The secret policeman.—Large print ed.—
Linford mystery library
    1. Murder—Investigation—Great Britain—Fiction
    2. Police—Investigation—Great Britain—Fiction
    3. Detective and mystery stories
    4. Large type books
    I. Title
    823.9'2 [F]

    ISBN 978–1–84782–302–1

Published by
F. A. Thorpe (Publishing)
Anstey, Leicestershire

Set by Words & Graphics Ltd.
Anstey, Leicestershire
Printed and bound in Great Britain by
T. J. International Ltd., Padstow, Cornwall

This book is printed on acid-free paper

To Mrs C. P. Oelfose:

*For her unconditional and unending faith and love.*

# 1

## The Criminal Intelligence Service

In April 1994, four years after his release from prison, Nelson Mandela became the first democratically elected president in South Africa. Three years later, his African National Congress government was struggling against a tidal wave of violent crime so serious that the Redevelopment and Construction Program had stalled, foreign investors were fleeing the country, and Johannesburg and Cape Town had become the second and third most dangerous cities in the world. In Durban, South Africa's third metropolis, there had already been nine hundred and two murders by June.

It was hardly surprising that one of the few thriving amidst the chaos in the city was a policeman, Jack Forrester. The son of a police major general, he had joined the South African Police Service as an officer entrant after completing his degree at university. Two years later he won the Police Cross for Bravery (Gold), the highest decoration in the SAPS. Now, with only five years service, he was — at twenty-six — already a senior superintendent. Last month he had received a second decoration, the Police Star for Merit, from the Minister of Safety and Security, Sydney Mafamadi. The award had made Forrester the highest decorated policeman in the country, and it was rumoured that Mr Mafamadi, the National Commissioner of the SAPS, and several other important men, were watching him. With his dark good looks, rugby three-quarter physique, and soft-spoken charisma, he was definitely on his way up in the world.

Forrester ran the Special Investigations Unit, a small internal affairs squad operating from C R Swart Square SAPS, the District Headquarters in central Durban. He had only six men under his command, four detectives and a Field Unit — two plainclothes policemen to do the legwork and make the arrests. His immediate superior was Director Morgan Subramanny, an Asian officer who reported to the District Commissioner in charge of the Square. From time to time, he would give Forrester a job that didn't strictly fall under the unit's aegis. Whether or not Subramanny told him, Forrester knew that nearly all of these were requests from either District Commissioner Smit, or Provincial Commissioner Ngidi, and as such gave them top priority.

Something about the summons he'd received this Monday morning put Forrester in mind of one of these jobs, and he wasn't happy about it: at present, his unit was working on two top priority cases. At the beginning of last week, he had been handed a videotape which was claimed to be evidence of four Metropolitan Police dog handlers torturing suspects with their dogs. The four policemen were white, the three suspects black, there was nothing more to say. A few days later, however, a matter of even graver importance was handed to him. A police station in the violent suburb of Ntuzuma was closing. On the last day of the police exit, workmen were removing fittings when they found fifteen case dockets literally stashed under the carpet. All were for murder. Forrester had lost several of his own men in Ntuzuma while serving in the Internal Stability Unit, so he'd given the videotape to his Field Unit, and put all four detectives on the murder dockets.

This time, as he climbed the concrete stairs to the ninth floor, he was determined to stick to his guns: he couldn't afford to — or wouldn't — drop the manpower assigned to either of his two cases.

'Hello, Jack, sit down, sit down.'

'Good morning, Morgan.' Forrester sat.

'How are you, this morning?'

'Busy.'

'Of course, of course. I suppose you're wondering why I've called you up here so early this morning.'

'I'm rather hoping it's not to give my unit any more work . . . sir.'

'Well, it's funny you should say that, Jack, but I do have a job for you — direct from the Provincial Commissioner. It won't interfere with your unit, but.'

'No?' Forrester found that hard to believe.

'No. The DC's asked for a detective to assist the CIS, and Mr Ngidi wants you to do the job.' The Criminal Intelligence Service was the name the SAPS gave to the former Security Branch, the dreaded political police of the *apartheid* years.

'But Morgan, come on, you know what I'm working on.' Forrester stood up. He knew that any job with the CIS would supersede all current work. He could see the Met and Ntuzuma cases going on the backburner indefinitely.

'No, no, no,' Subramanny was waving his palms in the air, 'you just wait and be listening to me.' Forrester sat back down, and let the director talk. 'All DC Smit told me was that the case involves the murder of a CIS man. He and Mr Ngidi both want your help: they want *you*, personally, Jack. It's in honour of you. It won't affect the functioning of the unit because they just want one man — and I'm going to be looking after your boys anyway.'

Two things sprang to Forrester's mind immediately: he doubted Subramanny's competence to look after his unit; and taking him from his squad *would* effect their functioning — unlike some officers he didn't just sit and supervise. He decided not to mention either. 'So I'm going to be attached to the CIS. Do you know how long they want me for?'

'No, my friend, you're not going there, they're coming here.'

'Excuse me?'

'Yes, Jack, they're sending your partner over this morning,' he checked his watch, 'he'll be here in an hour.'

'But I'm to work only on the CIS case?'

'Yes, yes, of course.'

'So this guy's going to have to be given a space in our office? I hope he's bringing his own desk.'

'No, the two of you will be using this office.'

'Your office?'

'Yes, Jack. I volunteered it to DC Smit. You and I will swap desks,' he laughed.

'Why?'

'Privacy, your office is no good with the

seven of you sharing four desks. Inspector Jackson wanted you and him to have some privacy. The Provincial Commissioner wants a man who knows when to keep his mouth shut, Jack. A man with . . . tact.'

Forrester didn't think his unit would be too happy to be sharing their office with Subramanny. 'But surely that's no good for you, Morgan, you've too much confidential work yourself to use my office.'

'Never you be minding, Jack, I'll make a plan. In the mean time, you're right, I do have plenty of work, so you just solve this case quickly, and then we can both get back to our jobs. Okay?'

Forrester knew he had no choice. Reluctantly, he rang the charge office on the ground floor, and arranged for a couple of constables to come up and help him and Subramanny move the director's files down a floor.

By half-past nine, he'd settled into his new workplace. Subramanny had emptied the desk and left a filing cabinet with three drawers empty. There were two comfortable chairs and a second phone had been procured. Given that he was going to be dealing with the CIS, Forrester wondered if the filing cabinet wouldn't stay empty. A phone call announced that Inspector Jackson was on his way up. Forrester placed a second key to the office next to the phone Jackson would be using, and waited.

'Superintendent Forrester?'

'*Ja*, you must be the inspector from Aliwal Street.'

'Yes, sir: Jackson.' They both had firm handshakes.

'Jack Forrester. Jackson?'

'Just Jackson.'

For a second, Forrester thought Jackson was saying his name was Justin, then he realised that he just didn't want to be called by anything other than his surname. Nice. A good start to their working relationship.

Inspector Jackson was of medium height, with broad shoulders and a strong build. He had short, brown hair and a light brown goatee, neatly-trimmed. A dark purple scar about half a centimetre thick and ten long ran diagonally down his left cheek. He wore a blazer, an open-necked shirt, and chinos.

'Sit down. This'll be our office. There's your key,' he indicated the desk as he sat down, 'and everything in here is empty,' he said, gesturing towards the filing cabinets.

Jackson placed a Crime Administration System docket on the desk. It was thin, and none of the usual information had been filled in on the front cover. Jackson looked around the office, then nodded, 'Good.'

'So . . . what can I help you with?'

'This,' Jackson pushed over the docket. 'I'd like you to familiarise yourself with the information there. I'm going for a walk,' he smiled, 'I'll be back by the time you've finished.' He walked out, closing the door behind him. Forrester wasn't used to being treated with such disdain by his subordinates, but he had a feeling that although Jackson wasn't even an officer, he'd be the one leading the investigation.

Forrester opened the anonymous docket.

It was as slim as it looked, with only twenty loose pages and a sealed brown envelope. All of the pages were photocopies, and they appeared to be in a logical order. Forrester picked up the envelope. It didn't have a label either, but it was obvious it contained photographs. He put it to one side and began with the reports.

The first surprise was that the sparse sheets actually did concern the murder of a policeman; the second, that it had occurred in La Lucia, a suburb adjacent to where Forrester lived. The murder had happened a week ago, and yet he hadn't heard or read anything about it. The facts of the case were that last Tuesday, just after ten in the morning, the body of Superintendent Michael Baston of the CIS had been discovered at 5 Fairwood, the police house where he'd been living. His body was found by one of his men, who had been despatched to find Baston when he'd failed to arrive for work or respond to calls.

The body was found in the supine position in one of the spare rooms, with three stab wounds to the left hand side of

10

the chest. The knife, a stainless steel Wilkinson kitchen knife of the type used to slice meat, was found under the single bed in the same room. Two of the strikes from the knife had bounced off his ribs, but one had punctured the heart. Death was believed to have been instantaneous, or very close to it. There was a note referring to the photos at this point, and Forrester opened the brown envelope.

There were thirty-six photographs showing, variously, the body, crime scene, parts of the house and property, and Fairwood road. Forrester started with the shots of the body, cross-referencing as he continued. Baston had been wearing a white, long-sleeved shirt, which was unbuttoned to the chest, and khaki trousers. He was barefoot. A large pool of blood lay next to the body. It appeared that the body hadn't been moved after the murder and also that Baston hadn't dragged himself or struggled much after the knife had pierced his heart. Instantaneous, indeed.

A photograph of the knife, found under the bed near the body, showed a razor sharp blade of about twenty centimetres in length. No fingerprints had been found on either the blade or the handle. The knife may have belonged to Baston, but was usually sold as part of a set, which, with the absence of any prints, led the investigating officer to decide that it was probably brought to the house by the murderer. The time of death had been estimated at around eight o'clock or so the previous evening.

The main bedroom had been searched, and Baston's wallet and watch were missing. The bed was made, although it looked as if someone had been lying on top of the sheets. The gun safe had been opened and both of Baston's 9mm service pistols, a Glock and a Beretta, were missing. Nothing else was believed to have been stolen. The rear door of the house, which led to an enclosed patio and a small outhouse, had been forced with a crowbar. The crowbar was believed to have come from his Toyota Camry, which was still in the garage. The boot had been left open, and the felt cover of the spare wheel lifted. Other than a jack, a box of a hundred rounds of 9mm ammunition had been found.

The report stated that the door of the house had clearly been forced from the inside, with damage done to the exterior of the door afterwards. The crowbar had been left on the floor inside the door, in the kitchen. The photos confirmed the forced exit, as opposed to entry. The crowbar, house, and car had all been dusted for fingerprints, but there were none other than Baston's own, and those of a domestic servant, Dolly Cele, who cleaned and ironed every Tuesday and Thursday. Cele had been at her home in A Section, Kwa Mashu, on Monday night. There were various witnesses to confirm this, and her statement added nothing to the investigation.

Forrester thought the fingerprint results strange, and made a mental note.

The neighbours from the house on the corner with Oakleigh Drive had stated that they heard a car arrive at about seven-thirty in the evening. It had left about an hour later, but they hadn't seen it. The rest of the occupants of the small cul-de-sac were interviewed, but no one had seen or heard anything. Forrester noted that there was absolutely no information about Baston himself in the docket.

He made another mental note, and heard Jackson enter. Forrester ignored him. There was little else of use and after familiarising himself with the photos of the road, which he'd driven past numerous times, he looked up at Jackson. 'What, exactly, do you want me to do with this docket, Inspector Jackson?'

'Two things: keep it to yourself, and find the murderer.'

'So, you're going to provide me with the missing information?'

Jackson smirked, inadvertently flexing the scar, 'I'll provide as much as I can — sir.'

Forrester wondered how recent the scar was, and how it had been acquired. 'I thought I'd been selected for this particular job because my superiors consider me discreet; is that not so?'

'Don't ask me why you were chosen, I haven't got a clue.'

'So, I'm not going to get the information I need to investigate the case?'

'Superintendent, I'll give you all I'm cleared to give. *My* superiors want the murderer found; I'm here to help — not hinder — you.'

Forrester snorted, 'I'll be the judge of that. You haven't exactly got off on the right foot, Inspector. First, why have I been given this docket a week after the murder? What's the point of giving me a cold case — it's probably too late to find the killer now.'

'It's CIS policy to investigate our own. After a week on the case, the investigating officer was able to rule out the possibility that Superintendent Baston's murder had anything to do with his current assignments. We don't have the resources available to pursue this, so you've been chosen to do it for us — with my help.'

'You investigated the case?'

'No.'

'Then what good are you to me? Why are you here?'

'Because you need a liaison, and I was chosen.'

'And you expect me — the two of us — to solve this case without involving any other policemen?'

'*Ja*, those are my orders.'

'This is ridiculous,' Forrester shook his head, 'your superiors expect me to solve this with one hand tied behind my back after it's already a week old. How long do they expect me to work on this?'

'I don't know.'

'You bloody find out for me. My unit's working on two top priority cases at the moment, and this,' he slammed his palm on the docket, 'means that they're one man short! But before you do that you can answer a second question: who the hell was this Superintendent Baston? I've been given absolutely zero to go on; it's completely unacceptable . . . '

Jackson sat down, raising his palm to placate Forrester. 'I know, I know. If you give me a minute I'll tell you all the background information I've been cleared to pass on. Not just about the superintendent, but also his last assignment.'

'By all means . . . '

# 2

## The Azanian People's Liberation Army

Forrester had serious doubts about the truth of what Jackson was telling him, but he suspended disbelief long enough to hear the man out and to make note of questions he thought might be answered.

On the 21$^{st}$ May Superintendent Michael Baston had returned to Durban from America, where he had spent the last eighteen months on foreign duty. He'd taken over the CIS's pursuit of the rogue elements of APLA that had refused to integrate into the Defence Force. The pursuit was a nationwide CIS directive, and in Durban was being run in conjunction with SANAB, the South African Narcotics and Alcohol Bureau, the SAPS's Drug Squad.

During the *apartheid* years the African National Congress and other socialist political parties included paramilitary groups responsible for guerrilla warfare on South African soil. When Nelson Mandela was arrested in 1962, he was in fact head of *uMkhonto we Sizwe*, the ANC's armed wing. When he'd been released twenty-eight years later, he'd ordered all paramilitaries to cease activity in order to allow the political solution to take its course. Most had complied, but the Azanian People's Liberation Army — APLA — the armed wing of the Pan-African Congress, were a notable exception.

Cells continued terrorist attacks right up to the democratic elections in 1994. After the ANC's success in the elections, Mandela was appointed president, and began absorbing the paramilitaries into a new National Defence Force. Again, many APLA members disobeyed the order to join. Some went overseas to try and drum up support for their militant anti-European stance, while others infiltrated organised crime groups to continue their struggle. It wasn't long before APLA became an embarrassment to their former brothers in arms and the CIS were given the task of arresting all dissidents still operating in South Africa.

The case that had resulted in Superintendent Baston's return to Durban had really begun in February when there were two shootings in two nights in the Point area of Durban. Both incidents involved oriental men. Five men working as enforcers for local drug dealers and pimps were killed or wounded, and it was believed that attacks were orchestrated by a man named Yusuf Mannikum, who lived nearby in West Street. Mannikum, a former APLA member, was known to be providing prostitutes for Chinese sailors, and was being watched by SANAB for suspected drug trafficking.

The investigation was led by Captain van Niekerk, of SANAB, but because of Mannikum's APLA connection, Inspector Robert Baston — the superintendent's younger brother — was assigned as well. At this stage it was suspected that Mannikum was providing a base for a slowly growing Triad presence in the Point.

In April the CIS were involved in a

shoot-out with two Chinese men in Newlands West. Unfortunately both men were killed by the police and little information was gained. The arrest of four of Mannikum's men for possession of heroin later that month had blown the case wide open: Mannikum was arrested and connected to Michael David, an Asian man from Reservoir Hills. David was believed to be trafficking in heroin, and supplying arms to extremist Moslem groups in Morocco, Algeria, Spain, and Britain. He was also alleged to have contacts with Pakistani criminals in London. Unfortunately, the CIS had to release Mannikum shortly after his arrest, but as he had provided the link with David, it was a minor setback.

On the night of Wednesday 12th of May, however, Captain van Niekerk was shot dead in his police quarters in Durban North. The following night, Inspector Baston had been killed in his house in Bellair. The assassin had set fire to the house and been chased by police before escaping. The two policemen were the most important men in the investigation, and there were no doubts as to the motive for their murder. The assassin was found in Johannesburg a week later, where he was killed by the CIS while resisting arrest. His name was Mark Zaoui and he was a British Moslem.

Superintendent Baston was recalled from his duties in America and, upon his return, took over the investigation, which now included the murder of his younger brother. On the 30th May, Baston seized a large consignment of heroin and re-arrested Mannikum. Two days later, with the assistance of Special Task Force police commandos, Baston and his team raided a property owned by David. Two suspects were killed in the raid and two wounded. One of the wounded suspects was employed by Mannikum, while the other was a Triad, wanted for various crimes by the Chinese police. Baston had recovered heroin, weapons, and ammunition to a total value of nearly a million rand.

Five days later, he was able to secure a warrant of arrest for David, but David fled before he was able to serve it. Baston had spent the weekend before his death covering airports and harbours that David might have used to escape. He hadn't been successful, however, and David was at large.

Baston had taken last Monday off and was due to return to work on Tuesday morning. His failure to return to work led to the discovery of his body at the house in Fairwood. The house was a police safe-house, and it had been given to Baston to provide him with accommodation on his return from America.

Jackson paused in his delivery to give another of the dry coughs that made Forrester think he must be a smoker. Michael Baston was thirty-six when he was killed. He had been in the SAPS for sixteen years and the CIS for the last ten. Jackson wouldn't go into any details about his postings, except that he'd worked in Cape Town up to the end of 1993, then been moved to Durban. He'd left Durban for America in November 1995. While in Durban he'd lived in Glen Anil, a suburb to the west of La Lucia, with which Forrester was also familiar. Baston was single, with no children, and had spent all of his time since his return pursuing Mannikum and David.

Jackson coughed again, cleared his throat, and was silent.

Forrester believed very little of what he'd heard, but gave no indication of his scepticism. Instead, he asked for contact details of Michael Baston's friends and family. Jackson replied that Baston had no living family, and gave him the names of two colleagues from Aliwal Street, Captains Menye and van der Westhuizen. Forrester was sure that the CIS captains would've already been briefed to reveal no more than Jackson already had. He wouldn't waste his time with them. He decided to try something else instead. 'I'm going to require a photograph of each of the brothers. The most recent you can find.'

'Each? Both . . . '

'*Ja*, a photograph of Robert and a photograph of Michael. ASAP.'

'Why do you . . . '

'ASAP, Inspector,' Forrester cut him

off. 'Now, I'm required in court shortly. After that I'll be off to the crime scene. I will see you here tomorrow morning at eight.'

'But . . .'

'That will be all, Inspector,' Forrester stood, picked up the docket and his jacket, and walked briskly out the door.

Five minutes later, he was driving his metallic grey Ford Telstar north on the M4 Northern Freeway. He took off his tie and undid his top button. Both he and Jackson knew there was no court appearance, but Forrester couldn't care less. He had to rid himself of the man for a while and think the whole story through. He suspected that Jackson might try to follow him so he put his foot down, speeding over the Umgeni River in the overtaking lane, before pulling in sharply left for the off-ramp at the fourth junction. He ignored the hooting from behind and cut hard left onto Old Mill Way. By the time he reached Northway, he was certain that he was now alone, whether or not he'd been followed from the Square.

Forrester drove up Northumberland Place, turning into the driveway at number twenty. His parents' house was a large double-storey, set on three-quarters of an acre of land, and divided into three gardens by high walls. Forrester parked at the bottom of the driveway, knocked on the door, and used his own key to unlock the burglar-guard gate while he waited. His father answered.

Major General Forrester had retired from the SAPS in 1994 after thirty-five years of service. He was from London and had joined the SAPS as a constable, working his way up to being the highest ranking non-native in the entire armed forces. Three years on, at fifty-eight, he still stood ramrod straight, and was lean and broad, with iron grey hair.

After exchanging pleasantries with the old man, Forrester found his mother, both grey and healthy like her husband, and Esmeralda, their maid. Both were well and it wasn't very long before he and his father were settled in the lounge with cups of percolated coffee.

'So how are you, Dad?'

'Good, boy, good. What's on your mind?' The general had retained his English accent, despite all the years in South Africa.

Forrester smiled, 'You can tell, then?'

'Of course I can. You sometimes forget I've known you for twenty-six years. Tell me.'

'What can you tell me about the Criminal Intelligence Service?'

'Two things: it's the politically correct name for the Security Branch, and don't get involved with them.'

'I knew the first, and I don't have any choice in the second.'

'Why?'

'The Provincial Commissioner has given me the job of investigating the murder of a superintendent in the CIS which happened last Monday in a not-so-safe-house in La Lucia. I'm working with one of their inspectors.'

The general sighed. 'That's a shame, boy. It won't do your career any good by getting involved with them. Not even now that the government's changed.'

'I'm afraid I don't have a choice, Dad.

But it's just one murder. The sooner I solve it, the sooner I can get back to my job. What I wanted was your opinion on the likelihood of SAPS involvement overseas. I've been told that this superintendent has spent the last eighteen months in America. I don't believe it. What do you think?'

'The CIS has a long history of missions to foreign countries, as did the various executive units of military intelligence before the government changed.'

'I know that, but I mean now.'

'You know that?'

'*Ja*, I know what it was like during the *apartheid* years.'

'Are you sure?'

'What do you mean?'

'Did you know that the ANC's London offices were bombed by the Security Branch in 1982, for instance?'

'I'd heard a rumour to that effect, but I always thought it must have been the Defence Force. Policemen don't go planting bombs . . . do they?'

'They did in South Africa. Would it surprise you to learn that the Star for

Outstanding Service was awarded to the brigadier, major, four captains, and warrant officer involved in the bombing?'

'Really?'

'Oh yes. There were various other foreign missions in the eighties, most of which were kept confidential. At the end of 1985, the Security Branch tried to recruit me.'

'You?'

'Yes. We were in Pretoria and I was a colonel at the time. They came to the house one night; you and Rosemary stayed upstairs with your mother. They wanted me to go to East Germany for them.'

'East Germany!'

'Yes. That's why they wanted to recruit me: because I was still a British citizen, and because I spoke German. I think I might have received an overture in 1981 for the London bombing, but I always made it clear that I wasn't a political policeman. And so should you. Look at what happened to Louis Botha.'

Louis Botha was a friend of the

general's, a major in the CIS who had been charged with treason for supporting the ANC's rivals in the lead-up to the 1994 elections. The case was still being heard at the Durban and Coastal Supreme Court.

'Well, I'm not, but it's different now that the government has changed.'

'It's different, but it's still not safe to involve yourself with politics if you're a policeman. Governments change. If you've spent your career supporting a government instead of fighting crime, you won't know where you stand. Every government wants policemen and soldiers to do its dirty work; and every opposition that takes power hangs those men out to dry. Look what's happened here. It'll be exactly the same in Britain when the IRA get what they want.'

Forrester felt that his father was straying off topic, 'No, what I mean is: now. Do you think that the CIS have operatives abroad?'

'Yes.'

'Do you just think that, or know it?'

'It's more than an educated guess, but

the last evidence I have is the assassination of the Govender family in Kanye, Botswana. That was in 1992.'

'Who were they?'

'Simeon Govender was an APLA terrorist. Him, his wife, and two sons, were all shot dead by the Security Branch across the border.'

Forrester was a little exasperated, 'But that was still before Mandela's government. Do you still think the CIS has people abroad now?'

'Boy, I wouldn't doubt it for a minute. And neither should you. You've been warned.' He smiled at his son, but he could see Forrester wasn't convinced. 'Was this CIS superintendent murdered because of the case he was working on?'

'I'm told that the CIS have spent a week looking into that and decided not.'

'And you believe them?'

'No. I don't know what it was, but my choices are: an assassination, a random act of violence, or — well, something else.'

'And the CIS have told you it's not an assassination, so that you don't ask awkward questions?'

'*Ja*, that's right.'

'Don't believe it. You know the statistics for murdered policemen. What was it last year, well over three hundred?'

'*Ja*, but . . . '

'Did I ever tell you an assassin was hired to kill me?'

'No. When?'

'In 1962. I was a constable on foot patrol around the Grey Street Market. I can only think that my predecessor must have been on the take because the illegal trading around the market was rife. I started issuing warnings and making arrests and got various offers to make it worth my while to look the other way. I arrested the first two traders that tried to bribe me, and continued enforcing the bylaws. After I'd been there about six weeks, a man I'd never seen before attacked me with an axe.'

'What happened?'

'Oh, he literally jumped out of an alley as I was doing my rounds. Luckily I spotted him out of the corner of my eye and ducked. I shot him in the stomach before he could get a second swing in.'

'Dead?'

'Well, it's a funny story actually. After I shot him, he threw the axe down and ran for Berea Station. I gave chase, but I couldn't get a second shot in because of all the bystanders. We didn't have radios on foot patrol in those days either, so I couldn't call for back-up until after I'd lost him somewhere on the tracks.

'I went back to the place where he'd attacked me, but someone had made off with the axe. Also, there was no blood — anywhere. My visiting sergeant thought I'd made the whole thing up. I got a reprimand when I tried to pursue it, so I made my own enquiries at the morgue. When the body of a black male with a stomach wound turned up there three days later I checked on it and found my man. Apparently, he'd jumped into a goods compartment on a cargo train headed to Pinetown. They found his body still on the train in the shunting yard a couple of days later. I was bloody glad, but I never got my apology from the sergeant.'

'Did you find out who'd hired him?'

'I knew who it was, although I couldn't prove it. It didn't matter, because they left me alone after that. All of them.'

Forrester wasn't surprised. 'And that was all over enforcing the city bylaws. Wow. Look, I must be off, I haven't even been to the crime scene yet. I just need to use your phone before I go.'

He dialled an office in the CIS headquarters at the Boland Bank Building in Aliwal Street. He got Captain Cray's answering machine, and then tried his cellular. He left a message on the latter asking the captain to call him when convenient.

Then he thanked his father for his advice, said goodbye to everyone, promised to pass all their regards to Delia, and took his leave.

# 3

## Murder in La Lucia

It was only a fifteen minute drive to La Lucia and Fairwood, but it was enough for Forrester to organise his thoughts. Although the general had a tendency to relate everything to his own experience, he did have thirty-five years of policing to fall back on. And he had just about seen and done it all in his time. Forrester had had no idea that the SAPS had been involved overseas to the extent described by his father. He was disgusted that policemen would plant bombs — it made them no better than the terrorists they despised — and proud of his father for keeping out of the CIS.

He knew he could solve some of the mystery by going through newspaper archives, but his initial impression was that Michael Baston didn't really exist. In fact, he was convinced of it. Inspector

Robert Baston had been allegedly murdered by an assassin on the 13<sup>th</sup> May. The assassin had conveniently set fire to the crime scene, no doubt charring the body beyond immediate recognition, and escaped.

Eight days later, the man's brother, Superintendent Michael Baston, appears out of the ether to take over the investigation. No relatives' details were given: no one to confirm whether there were one or two brothers. What utter nonsense. No birth or school details either. Again, no one to confirm whether there were one or two brothers. The whole thing was just ridiculous.

Just what did Jackson expect Forrester to believe Michael Baston was doing in America for eighteen months? No matter what his father said about the old days, the government had made it clear that the Secret Service were the sole foreign intelligence department. All security services were now strictly controlled by the Ministry of Intelligence, and the days of policemen and soldiers doing cloak-and-dagger work overseas were over. And even if his father's cynicism was correct and there were CIS members overseas, there was no way that any policeman would be allowed to investigate his own brother's death. It was all nonsense.

So, the first problem for Forrester was that he was actually investigating the murder of the resurrected Robert Baston. The second was that he couldn't work out why he'd been involved at all. According to Jackson, David had arranged Robert Baston's murder. David was now on the run. Wasn't there every chance that if he'd had one of the brothers murdered, he'd done the same to the other? Perhaps it was too late for David to go ahead with his trafficking, but it still seemed likely that he'd had the second — or resurrected — brother murdered out of revenge. If so, it was an organised crime matter, best dealt with by those who had been working the case from the beginning.

The name Michael David bothered Forrester. He'd heard it, or seen it, somewhere before. A briefing, a bulletin, a passing comment . . . he couldn't remember.

If it was an organised crime matter or related to renegade APLA paramilitaries — or both — why call him in? Even if the murder wasn't connected to Baston's work, why Forrester? Perhaps he was being set up. Two CIS men killed at their residences in two months: what was really going on that Jackson wouldn't tell him? Or maybe he was just being paranoid.

Forrester found 5 Fairwood easily, pulling up across the road. He took the photographs with him and entered the property. There was yellow tape wrapped around the spikes of the fencing, but no police presence. The front door was closed but unlocked. He began in the room where the murder had occurred, using the photos to place the body, murder weapon, and other clues no longer present. The pictures were expertly taken, and Forrester couldn't see that the photographer had missed anything.

Moving into each room, he paused, trying to imagine it as the temporary home of a policeman rather than an empty shell. One thing was for certain, it was quite obviously a temporary home. A safe-house, Jackson had said without irony. There were no signs of it belonging to anyone. No personal items: pictures, mementos ... the kind of things that seem to clutter all but the neatest houses. It could be explained by Baston only having been back in the country for two weeks. It could also be explained by Baston hiding his true identity.

After moving through all the rooms in the house, Forrester examined the back door. Once again the photos were accurate: it had obviously been forced from the inside, with a half-hearted attempt to damage the outside as well.

A cover-up?

A very poor one, if so. One of the poorest Forrester had ever seen, in fact. Why? If it was a cover-up, it seemed to open up several possibilities. Like the murderer being admitted to the house by Baston, and the possibility that it was someone he knew. Then the culprit broke out to make it look like a burglary gone wrong. Why break out and not in? He could have used the keys to open the door and forced the lock from the outside to make it more realistic.

An assassin, a policeman, even the most inept burglar, would have made a better job of a cover-up. Or was that the whole point? To make the cover-up so obvious that it became its own clue . . . An assassin would also have been likely to have come better armed. Forrester looked at the knives in the kitchen. It didn't appear that the weapon was from the house, but it was possible. There was a lot that was possible, but nothing probable or definite.

Yet.

Forrester went out to the patio at the back, and tried the outhouse. Nothing of any interest there. The garage was empty, the car having been removed. He went back into the house, sitting on the bed in the spare room. He looked at the dried blood beneath him and the photos of the body. The break-in was contrived. It was poor; it was obvious; it was amateur. It appeared that the murderer was known to the victim and had inexpertly attempted to make it look like a housebreaking and theft. The items stolen were another half-hearted attempt to mislead.

But the body itself wasn't stage-managed.

No. The murder had occurred just as it appeared in the photos. Was it planned, the knife brought here by the murderer, or spontaneous, the knife grabbed from the kitchen or wherever else it had been? Neither made sense to Forrester. It annoyed him that he couldn't provide a logical explanation, but there was something about the way Baston had been dressed and the amateurish nature of the cover-up that gave him a clue to the murderer's identity. It was nothing he could justify to Jackson, or even one of his own men, but he felt it provided a starting point for his efforts.

He spent another half hour just sitting on the bed, looking at the photos of Michael — or Robert — Baston, running scenarios through his head.

Forrester closed the gate and stood on the road. It was steep, with only a few houses on either side. Up the hill, Fairwood ended in a small turning circle, from which there was a steep footpath

40

leading through bush to the main road about a hundred metres beyond. Looking down, over Oakleigh Drive, he could see La Lucia Mall, with its recent extensions complete. Closest to Fairwood, stood the Health & Racquet Club, probably Durban's most upmarket gym. Beyond the club and the mall was the Indian Ocean. The road was quiet, and Forrester wondered if you could hear the sea at night.

There seemed little point in interviewing the neighbours, the CIS had already made a thorough job of it. He was just about to get back in his car, when he thought about the photos in his hand and remembered that Michael Baston, in death at least, had been very well-built. The open shirt had shown well-defined pectoral muscles, muscles that certainly hadn't come without sweat and sculpting. He doubted that the man would have had time to go to the gym since his return from America, but recalled that he'd previously lived in Glen Anil, a short distance away. He looked at the Health & Racquet Club: it was worth a shot. He put the photos in his boot, and walked down the hill.

The Health & Racquet was just starting to get busy, but Forrester managed to get the attention of one of the many young, tanned, and fit assistants. Michael Baston had indeed been a member. He'd joined in December 1993 and his membership had expired at the end of last year. Unfortunately, there was no record of when he had last used the facilities. Forrester asked the assistant if he'd known Baston himself and received a negative reply. He then asked if there was a record of who'd sold him the membership and was directed to one of the managers, a muscular blonde man in his early thirties.

The manager, Grant Melville, remembered Baston. He also told Forrester that Baston associated with a man named Steve Rich. Forrester asked Melville if that was Dave's brother, and he replied in the affirmative. Forrester had played rugby with Dave Rich at Northlands High School, and then against him in later years. He thought he'd met the brother once as well, but couldn't be sure. There was more. Michael Baston had, in the middle of 1995, been going out with Angela Broad, a woman Forrester had met. Forrester thanked Melville and left with the contact details for both the Rich brothers and Angela, all of whom were current club members.

He was starting to see why he might have been called in on the case. The murder was apparently unrelated to organised crime or Baston's work. That left either a random act of violence, or a friend or family member. The evidence pointed to the latter and the victim was a man who had either lived in Durban North or at least maintained an identity there. Forrester had lived in Durban North for the last ten years. Apparently, he and Baston had known some of the same people, perhaps moved in the same social circles.

*Ja*, it was starting to make sense.

He walked back up to Fairwood, past his car, and further up to the footpath. It took him all the way to William Campbell

Drive, one of the arterial roads between Durban North and Umhlanga. From William Campbell Drive he looked down to Fairwood, his car, the mall, the sea. There were plenty of places where one could sit comfortably in the bush and watch number five. And plenty of space to park a car on the soft shoulder.

Forrester wondered.

It was getting dark now, so he walked back down, got back in his car, and headed back to Durban North. He hadn't yet reached William Campbell Drive when his cell rang. It was Captain Cray. Forrester pulled over at Newlyn Centre and rang Cray's cell from the public phone.

Forrester's infrequent conversations with Cray were usually interesting, and today was no exception. Michael Baston had been a captain in the CIS when Cray had joined in the middle of 1994. Cray believed he was originally from the Cape Province. Inspector Robert Baston had transferred in to the Durban unit from the Pretoria CIS when his brother had left for America in November 1995. It was all Cray would reveal, except that he hadn't known either man personally. He and Forrester would meet tomorrow evening.

It was enough for Forrester: confirmation that the two brothers had never actually worked in the same place at the same time. That, in addition to the suspicious fire and the anomalies in the case. It was so obvious. What kind of idiot did Jackson take him for?

Forrester got back in his car and phoned Angela Broad before he drove off, arranging to meet her at her home in the morning. He tried Dave Rich as well, but couldn't get him on either of the two numbers, so left messages on both. Then he rejoined the long line of traffic heading south.

Forrester and his wife, Delia, lived in a recently developed part of Durban North called Riverside, above the north bank of the Umgeni River. They had bought the duplex brand new when they married, two years ago. The estate, on Queen's View, was called Queen's Heights, and consisted of about thirty terraced homes built on two levels and surrounded by a high wall. There were no gardens but each house had at least one garage. They'd been very happy with the home, one of the cheaper ones on offer with only two bedrooms and a single garage.

Forrester and Dee both liked Durban North, and the location on the riverbank gave them easy access to both places of work as well as Forrester's parents. Dee's own parents lived under Table Mountain in Cape Town, and her brother and sister had emigrated to Australia.

Emigration was something Forrester had been thinking about since he'd married Dee. He knew the life of a policeman was unfair on a wife, let alone a family. He thought of his poor mother with a father, husband, and son all — at one stage or another — policemen. The years of worry showed in the lines on her face.

He also knew that he could join South Africa's brain drain and sell his degree overseas for a lot more money than he was earning in the police, even as a senior superintendent. Both of these things had tugged at his conscience before, but he and Dee hadn't made a decision yet. There didn't seem any rush, although two out of his three closest friends from university were already settled abroad, one in London and one in Auckland. His younger sister, Rose, had been living in London for eighteen months already. She was in two minds about whether to come back or stay, but Forrester thought it inevitable that she'd stay.

At the moment he and Dee were content where they were. She worked in a travel agency in Musgrave Centre, which enabled them to take advantage of the best offers and travel more than their salaries dictated. And Forrester's career — for the moment, at least — was unstoppable. It was one success after the next. Would he, one day, be the Minister of Safety and Security himself? Would it be him conferring medals on brave young policemen and telling their wives how proud he was? Forrester was only twenty-six. Even if it took him twenty years to get to Mr Mafamadi's position, he'd be younger than the man was now. And surely it would be less than twenty years, not more?

There was only one thing that would make him think seriously about emigrating soon: if Dee was pregnant. Forrester didn't think that South Africa, even in Durban North, was any place to raise a child. Although what opportunities the child of a senior government minister would have, he didn't know. They might be endless . . .

He used the remote to enter the estate and smiled as he saw Dee in the garage, still getting out of the car.

It was good to be home.

# 4

## Michael Baston

Jackson was waiting in their office at eight o'clock on Tuesday morning. If he was annoyed at having been dumped the previous day, he didn't show it. As soon as Forrester sat down, he handed over two photos. Forrester saw an emotion in the hard, scarred face. Fear? He wasn't sure, but whatever it was, it was gone in an instant.

Both the photos were of a passport or ID size, blown up to about half A5. One was black and white, one colour. Forrester turned them over: the dates were written on the back. He very nearly burst out laughing, but allowed none of his feelings to show. *Jislaaik*, no wonder Jackson had been reluctant to provide him with them: they were so obviously the same man.

The colour photo was allegedly a shot

of Michael Baston taken last month. He had a chiselled, tanned face with a long blonde fringe and a close-trimmed blonde beard. The black and white photo, dated January 1987, was an ID shot for a police warrant card. But Robert Baston was quite clearly the same man. In the older photo he was younger, with a heavier face, clean shaven, and wearing his police tunic. Forrester couldn't believe that Jackson had just blithely handed over proof of such an amateur deception.

He kept his thoughts to himself once again, however, thanked the inspector, and updated him on his trip to the Health & Racquet Club and the interview at nine o'clock. Jackson seemed pleased with his progress.

Half an hour later they were heading north on the freeway in Forrester's Telstar. Angela lived in Sunningdale, the suburb immediately north of Glen Anil, in a simplex development in Fig Tree Rise. After a short search, they found the house and Forrester knocked on the door. It was opened by a muscular man of medium height, with blonde hair and a dark tan. He was the same age as Forrester, but his model face and body made him look younger. He extended a large, strong hand.

'*Howzit*, Jack.'

'Hello Dave, *howzit* going? I didn't expect to see you here. This is Inspector Jackson, a colleague of mine.' Dave nodded and shook Jackson's hand.

'Come in guys, I'll get Ange.' The policemen were shown to a small, tastefully-furnished lounge, and seated themselves on a long couch. Moments later Angela entered the room. She was short, shapely, and voluptuous, with long, straight, raven-black hair and a dark skin which belied her Mauritian origins. She was wearing a short, dark green dress, and her bright red lipstick matched the colour of her long nails. Both men stood up.

'Hello, Angela,' said Jack, extending his hand. 'We've met before. I'm Jack Forrester. I went to school with Dave and I'm a superintendent with the police now. This is my colleague, Inspector Jackson.'

She shook both their hands and sat

down opposite them, next to Dave. Dave spoke first. 'I got your message last night, Jack, and then when Angela told me that you'd arranged to see her as well, I thought I'd hang about.'

'No problem. How's your brother?'

'Fine, thanks, but he's away on business — in Jo'burg — at the moment. Why, do you want to see him as well?'

'*Ja*, when is he due back?'

'The end of the week, I think; Friday.'

'I'll have to wait, then. Angela, I'm not sure if . . . well, I'm sorry, did you go out with a man named Michael Baston, two years ago?'

'Yes, why?'

'A policeman?'

'Yes.'

'When was the last time you saw him?'

'Um . . . we broke up in July . . . ninety-five. I probably saw him a few times at the gym after that . . . but not in private or anything . . . I don't know, perhaps August or September. Why?'

'Well, I don't know if you were close or not, but I'm afraid to say that he was murdered last week.'

'Oh!' She seemed surprised, but not upset.

'I thought he was overseas?' said Dave.

'You knew him?'

'I'd seen him around once or twice. Steve was friends with him, and of course I knew he was Ange's ex.'

'When was the first time you met him?' Forrester asked Dave.

'Oh, er, maybe 1994? I'm not a hundred percent sure. He and Steve hadn't been mates for long, but I remember Steve saying that he'd gone overseas at . . . well, probably just after Ange said she last saw him.'

'Did you ever see him? I mean at the gym, or out and about?'

'*Ja*, I used to see him regularly at the gym. I'd say hello to him, but we weren't pals or anything.'

'Are you still playing rugby?'

'*Ja*, still at Crusaders.'

'Did you ever see him there?'

'No.'

'Or anywhere else, locally or in town?'

'No, I didn't.'

'Angela, what can you tell us about him?'

'Well, what do you mean?'

'Apparently no one knew Michael was back in the country. Obviously someone knew, otherwise he wouldn't be dead, but I'm looking for leads as to his friends and associates. Can you tell me who he mixed with, where he liked to go?'

'It's funny you should say that, you know, Jack, because no, I don't really know much about him. We went out for . . . about nine months . . . but I can't say you'd call us close. He was very private.'

'Did you meet his family?'

'No, but he said his parents were in Knysna and that he had a brother who was also a cop.'

'Did you meet them, the parents or the brother?'

'No.'

'Did he meet your parents?'

'Yes, I was living with my mom at the time. Dave and I only moved in together at the beginning of this year.'

'What about friends. Did you meet any of his friends, colleagues?'

'No, not colleagues. He never talked about work. Sometimes I wouldn't hear from him for a few days and he'd just say he'd been working. I know he worked in Cape Town before he moved here.'

'Did you know what work he did, in the police I mean?'

'Yes, he said he was a detective.'

'Do you know where he worked?'

'Um, in the main police station . . . the one on the freeway.'

'C R Swart Square?'

'Yes, that's it.'

'He didn't actually. Did you ever meet any of his colleagues?'

'I met a black guy he worked with a few times. Um, his name was Siza . . . I think.'

'Siza Menye?'

'It could have been. Nice guy, well-spoken, big-build.' Forrester glanced at Jackson, who nodded. Forrester continued, 'Friends, associates?'

'Well, Dave's brother, Steve. I know they were friends. There was also this doctor from Umhlanga, Steven Andrews. A funny guy, I didn't really like him.'

'Do you know where he lived?'

'Only Umhlanga somewhere.'

'And that was all as far as friends went?'

'Yes, just the other cop, Steve, and Steven.'

'Where was Michael living when you were with him?'

'He had a house around the corner from here, in Glen Anil; Pigeonwood.'

'His own?'

'I think so.'

'Where did he take you, where did the two of you go out?'

'It's funny really; we didn't seem to go out much, not when I think about it. We spent most of our time at his house . . . ' Forrester noticed a look of discomfort on Dave's face ' . . . we went to the Pig and Whistle, across from here, and he liked The Langoustine and the Beef and Barrel.'

'Anywhere else?'

'Not really. The occasional movie at the mall — and pizza. He liked pizza.'

'What about you, Dave, anything to add to what Angela knew about him?'

'No, didn't know the guy. I'll try and get you in touch with my brother, if you

56

like. He should be answering his cell some time during the day.'

'*Ja*, in fact, I'll just take all your details again to make sure I can contact you if I need to. There's just one more thing: where were the two of you last Monday night, between seven-thirty and eight-thirty?'

'Jesus, Jack, we were at school together! How can you justify asking me that!'

'Because, Dave, if I ask you now, it eliminates you from the investigation. I might be on the case today, but tomorrow it could be anybody's. If this goes to Murder and Robbery, you could find some bad boys on your doorstep making life very unpleasant. But if I've already covered all the bases, you've got less chance of being hassled.'

Dave didn't seem happy, but Angela piped up, grinning, 'That's easy,' she said, 'I finished at the gym at about quarter past seven. I went to visit my friend Jo in Pasadena, and then came back here. I was back before nine.'

'Dave?'

'Crusaders bar after work. I got back

here at about eight-thirty. But no one was bloody home, so I suppose that makes me a suspect?'

'No, of course not. If it becomes an issue, I'll ask the neighbours. Someone will have seen your car, or something. Don't worry about it.'

'I'm not: you are.'

'I'll take all those details now, please, including your friend's, Angela.'

There were decidedly fewer smiles and handshakes when the policemen left the house.

'You said he had no living relatives,' said Forrester as they climbed in the car, 'did the parents skip your mind?'

Jackson turned his head slowly. His tone was menacing: 'The parents were murdered in a home invasion last year. Are you trying to imply something?'

'I don't have to try.'

'Check the Knysna police records if you don't believe me. In the mean time, I respectfully suggest that you focus on the case . . . Superintendent.'

'I am,' replied Forrester.

'Where's Pasadena?' Jackson changed

the subject and the edge left his voice.

'It's a block of flats on the north side of the mall. You can see them from Fairwood.'

'Are we going there next?'

'You think she did it?'

'She was in the right place at the right time. But then so was he, depending on what time he left the bar.'

'*Ja*, we are going to go to Pasadena. Because after that we're going to start showing this photo around the places Angela mentioned — and a few others I know. But they're all restaurants or bars, so there's not likely to be anyone in until midday. Ring up Jo. Pasadena first — if she's in — and then we'll go back to the Square. We'll try and track down this Dr Andrews, then we'll make a copy of this photo and divide my list of likely spots in two. We'll show the photo around, see if we can put him with any people more recent than the lovely Angela.'

'We're looking for a chick?'

'Or guy. Anyone who might have seen him since he got back.'

Angela's friend Jo wasn't in, and she

didn't answer her cell. Forrester was grateful, because he desperately needed time to think. As they drove back to the Square, he replayed the conversation with Angela in his head.

How convenient that Baston's parents were dead — and recently, after his involvement with Angela. It was one more thing Forrester would need to check. One man could use dual identities to great advantage in the murky world of the CIS, or was he just letting his imagination run away with him? Possible. Except for the photos. The photos were hard evidence that the two men, supposedly seven years apart in age, were quite obviously one and the same. It didn't take a detective to see that man had just grown a bloody beard and shed a few kilos.

And Jackson's nervousness when he'd handed the photos over. He'd known he was playing into Forrester's hands, but couldn't do anything about it without arousing further suspicion. What Forrester really needed to do was show Angela both photos. In the nine months she was with the man, she might have seen him without his beard. Forrester thought he'd wait until he'd seen Cray. Cray, he had no doubt, would be able to tell him whether the two brothers were the same man, even if he wasn't prepared to reveal anything more.

# 5

## People Against Gangsterism and Drugs

Back at their office, Jackson tracked down Dr Andrews, only to find he was on holiday: a cruise to Madagascar which had started on Saturday. Meanwhile, Forrester left a message on Steve Rich's cell phone and drew up two lists. He was careful to put all the places he thought it likely that Baston might have frequented on his own. Jackson's were all long shots, except for the Beef and Barrel. Also, they were all likely to take more time. Forrester had included a return to the Health & Racquet Club, as well: he needed to get the CIS man out the way for a while. They left the office after lunch, agreeing to meet back at five o'clock.

Forrester wanted rid of Jackson for two reasons. First, he intended to show both photos to the people he interviewed.

Second, he had some research to do before they met, and before he met Captain Cray that night.

He drove straight back to the Pig and Whistle in Sunningdale. No joy: Baston had been seen, but not since he'd brought Angela there. Then the Frog and Fiddler in Park Road, The Tavern, Paoulo's, and the Horse and Hound. He finally found what he wanted at The Langoustine. The manager, Matthew Harvey, remembered Michael Baston — he identified the colour photo — as a regular customer. He remembered seeing him with at least three women over the couple of years he'd been eating there.

Harvey couldn't remember the earliest woman, knew Angela by name, and gave a description of the last one Baston had brought there. She was young, short, athletic, tanned; very pretty, with no make-up, and short brown hair. Baston had last been here with her a couple of years ago. He remembered it clearly because it was his own birthday, the 3rd November 1995. Harvey had seen the same woman twice since, both times with a girlfriend. He couldn't give a description of the first, but said that the second had long blonde hair, and was also very attractive. Forrester noted everything down, took his contact details, and thanked him.

He crossed the river and headed west, for Musgrave Centre. He was tempted to pop in to Thomas Cook and say hello to Dee, but thought better of it in case he was being followed. He tried Legends, Circus Circus, and then Cotton Eye Joe's. Nothing. He checked his watch after the last: time to make his way back to the Square.

He drove back to C R Swart via Greyville, where he pulled into the offices of Natal Newspapers. The company ran both Durban daily's, the morning and evening papers, as well as both of the Sunday papers. All papers more than a month old were kept on microfilm. He had an hour and a half to find what he wanted.

He began six months back, with an article on the increase in the small Chinese community in the Point, legal, illegal, and criminal. The community was contrasted with the Taiwanese community based in Durban North, made up almost entirely of very successful and hard-working business people. Next, Forrester found a set of articles about the two shootings in as many nights on the Point, both involving Chinese men. There was no mention of Yusuf Mannikum.

There was nothing for March, but an article in April confirmed that two Chinese gangsters had indeed been killed in a shoot-out with police in Newlands West, as Jackson had described. The article connected the men to the troubles on the Point, and mentioned organised crime and drug trafficking. Murder and Robbery and SANAB were reported as investigating. There was no mention of the CIS. An editorial followed and then a piece on the work of SANAB, and how the drug scene in Durban had changed dramatically in the last two years.

The articles that Forrester really wanted to see were next.

The *Natal Mercury* dated 20th May ran an article on the murder of Captain

Andries van Niekerk the previous night in Jim Fouche Avenue, across the road from Durban North SAPS. Captain van Niekerk had been found dead at midnight by a police constable from the charge office. His wife, calling from their home in Port Shepstone, had become concerned when she couldn't contact him. She had phoned the charge office and asked if they could send someone round to have a look.

The constable had found van Niekerk's body in the lounge. He'd been shot three times: head, chest, and left arm. There were signs of a struggle. The neighbours, all police families, hadn't heard anything suspicious. Van Niekerk was described as a detective with SANAB responsible for the ongoing investigations on the Point. Murder and Robbery were investigating. Still no mention of the CIS. The *Daily News* added little to the story.

The *Mercury* for the following day had an even longer article on the murder and arson in Hercules Close which followed the attack in Durban North. The neighbours had alerted the police after they'd heard several shots being fired. Shortly afterwards, the property had been set alight and a man had been seen getting into a green BMW. The police had arrived just as the BMW left the close and they chased it west on Sarnia Road, losing it in Stella Road after firing shots. Another patrol had picked the car up in Carrick Road, but had lost it in Chatsworth. The neighbours were unable to describe the man they saw getting into the car.

The body of Inspector Robert 'Birch' Baston was identified by his dental records. He was from the Cape Province and had been a policeman for ten years. He was based at C R Swart Square Detective Branch. There was a separate article connecting the two murders, but it seemed as if it had little — if any — factual basis.

Still no mention of the CIS: they were doing well.

The *Daily News* article added that the BMW was a hired car which had been rented by a foreign national on Tuesday. It was unclear as to whether or not the car had been stolen, or if the foreign national was a suspect. There was an editorial on the slaughter of policemen in South Africa, and statistics were quoted that showed 1997 was the second most dangerous year for policemen: a hundred and forty-four had already been killed nationwide. This was just behind the rate for 1996, when three hundred and forty-nine had been murdered or killed in the line of duty by the end of the year.

Forrester continued, paying careful attention to every day following the second murder.

On Thursday 28th May the *Daily News* ran a small article on a British man having been shot by police when they stopped him on his way to the airport. He had opened fire on the Murder and Robbery detectives and been shot dead. His name was Mark Zaoui and he was wanted for the murders of Captain van Niekerk and Inspector Baston in Durban the previous week.

The next relevant piece was in the *Mercury* on Monday 31st May. SANAB had, the previous day, arrested Yusuf

Mannikum, of West Street, Durban, when he was found in possession of a large quantity of heroin in a premises in Clare Hills. One of his men had been shot dead by police when he had failed to put down his handgun.

Yusuf Mannikum was believed to be a drug smuggler with links to the Chinese gangsters who had recently been in the news on the Point. Tuesday's *Daily News* ran a last-minute article on a second SANAB raid. This time, SANAB and the Special Task Force had raided a warehouse in Newlands West. A shoot-out had ensued, leaving a Chinese gangster dead. There were six arrests, including two other Chinese men connected to the troubles on the Point and Durban's harbour. For the first time, arms and ammunition were mentioned.

Which reminded Forrester about another part of Jackson's story he'd found difficult to believe yesterday.

There was nothing about Michael David or the raid on his house carried out the weekend before Michael Baston had been killed. The CIS still hadn't been mentioned and, perhaps more significantly, there was absolutely no mention of Superintendent Michael Baston.

Forrester finally found David's name in a short article in last Monday's *Daily News*: police were searching for Michael David, of Reservoir Hills, the Regional Coordinator of PAGAD, in connection with the trafficking of heroin.

That was where Forrester had heard the name before, PAGAD: People Against Gangsterism and Drugs. PAGAD was a Moslem vigilante organisation which had been founded last year in Cape Town by two men named Faroek Jaffer and Nadthmi Edries. Initially the group had organised armed patrols to discourage the drug dealers prevalent in the Moslem areas of Cape Town, claiming that this was necessary due to the corruption and inefficiency of the local police. A more sinister side was soon shown, however, when Rashaad Staggie, leader of the Hard Livings — the most notorious of the numerous local gangs — was shot and burned to death by PAGAD members.

At the beginning of this year, PAGAD

had staged a mass demonstration in Cape Town's city centre. The wives and daughters of the members had led the way and then, from behind them, shots were fired at police. Several people were wounded in the exchanges, and the government was now keeping a much closer eye on the group. A branch had sprung up in Durban, centred on the Randles Road Mosque in Sydenham. Due to the small size of the city's Moslem community, as well as an absence of gangs organised on the same scale as in Cape Town, however, PAGAD enjoyed only limited local support.

Forrester remembered the bulletin now, naming Michael David as the Regional Coordinator in Durban. It had come out after an incident with the police outside the Randles Road Mosque. Metropolitan Police officers had responded to a complaint of cars parked dangerously on the road. When they had ticketed the illegally parked vehicles, owners had emerged from the mosque and stoned them. The situation escalated, armed PAGAD members in shemags arrived, and there were several scuffles and a single arrest. Other than the problems associated with Michael David himself, however, this had been the only time that PAGAD had come to the attention of the Durban police.

There was no mention of Michael Baston's death. Or his life. Or anything about him at all. It was as if he hadn't existed. And that, thought Forrester, was because he never had. There was obviously a kernel of truth in the story that Jackson had told him, but no doubt there was a lot more to it. For a start, the inspector had forgotten to mention David's position in PAGAD. David was obviously a powerful and well-connected individual. He had his APLA allies, had used a British assassin to kill van Niekerk and Baston, and appeared to be allied to the Chinese Triads.

Just because the previous murders differed from the one in Fairwood, didn't mean that Michael Baston's death wasn't his doing. Perhaps he'd used one of his less-experienced PAGAD members, or perhaps the scene had been deliberately contrived in order to appear amateur.

That was more than a possibility. Was the amateur appearance of the crime the only basis on which the CIS had decided that Baston's death was unrelated to his work? If so, the ruse used by the assassin was entirely successful.

If it *was* a ruse.

The CIS had spent a week investigating the murder before deciding it wasn't anything to do with organised crime. They appeared to have been thorough. Maybe they were right and it wasn't connected. But Forrester decided that he couldn't afford to eliminate the revenge killing motive. He had to find out more about David. Cray would no doubt be helpful in that respect, but he had another line of inquiry he could pursue as well. Something closer to the source of his suspicions. He glanced at his watch: it would have to wait until tomorrow.

He was back in his office for five o'clock, but by quarter past, Jackson hadn't turned up yet. Either he'd found something, or the wild goose chase was taking him longer than Forrester had thought. Given his meeting in forty-five minutes, Forrester reflected that it was probably for the best. He left Jackson a note giving the description of the woman who'd been seen with Baston, and telling him he'd be in for eight tomorrow morning again. Then he switched off his cell — he didn't want Jackson asking him where he was — and left. The place he was going had no cellular reception anyway.

Forrester steered his car through the busy city centre towards the Southern Freeway, taking care to look for any signs of surveillance. There were none, which meant that if he was being followed, it was by experts.

The CIS was full of experts.

Forrester took the off-ramp for Edwin Swales VC Drive, heading to the Bluff. This southern suburb of Durban, perched atop the hill that gave it its name, was home to the exclusive Ocean View residential area and Marine Drive, as well as the Durban South police headquarters, and a National Defence Force Special Forces Brigade training centre. It was also where Captain Cray lived.

The sun had set by the time Forrester parked up in Foreshore Drive, at the southern end of Brighton Beach, and the northern tip of the Southern Coastal Park. The car park was poorly-lit and busy, but he made out Cray putting something in the boot of his white VW Jetta. Forrester opened his own boot and took out the bag with his running gear.

Chris Cray was a captain in the CIS. He had transferred from the Durban Dog Unit in 1994, where he'd been one of Durban's most successful uniform police-men. He and his dogs, first Declain and then Tanga, had appeared in the media numerous times for their exploits. Their most famous included the tackling of four suspects in a row at a theft on the freight railway, the single-handed arrest of a gang of thirteen armed robbers, and the apprehension of an AK47-wielding assail-ant in West Street Cemetery.

With his promotion to lieutenant at the end of 1995, Cray had joined a Captain Roma, his job consisting of the processing of all applications for marches, demon-strations, and protests, both legal and illegal. At least that was what Cray volunteered; Forrester had little doubt there was a lot more to it. Cray and Roma shared their office with Inspector Du Plessis, one of only three police photographers covering the entire Durban area. While the other two photographers covered crime scenes, Du Plessis worked solely for the CIS. Forrester had no doubt that the photographs of Fairwood were his expert handiwork.

Forrester had only worked with Cray once, but the result had been their recent joint award of the SAPS Star for Merit. Forrester had maintained a good working relationship with him ever since the incident. Cray had been a policeman for twelve years, and had a wealth of knowledge of all aspects of the job. In addition he was bright, taciturn, and — of course — an insider in the CIS.

Forrester shuffled into his shorts and vest in his car, and was lacing up his shoes when Cray appeared at the door. He was tall, slim, and slightly stooped. He had short blonde hair, a large, neat moustache, and seemed to give an impression of quiet intelligence. He was carrying a small rucksack. Forrester locked his car; put his gun, wallet, and keys in the rucksack; and the two men walked onto the sand.

The plan was to run south along the beach to the mouth of the Mlazi River, and then retrace their route back to Brighton. It was ten kilometres in total, a difficult run because it involved some wading and scrambling, depending on the tide. At night it could be dangerous, but there was already enough light from the three-quarter moon for the two men to see where they were going. Cray was older than Forrester, but he'd maintained the level of fitness he'd enjoyed as a dog handler. Although out of training himself, Forrester retained a residual stamina from his days as a provincial Under-21 rugby player.

They spent five minutes stretching and warming up, then set off south along the water's edge.

# 6

## Captain Cray Elucidates

Forrester waited until he and Cray had found a mutual, easy rhythm, and began telling him about his initial meeting with Jackson. He continued with the visit to the newspapers archive, the involvement of PAGAD — or at least a PAGAD member — and then his suspicions as to what had really happened.

Cray was silent throughout.

Forrester finished with a kilometre still left to go, and they ran on in silence. They stopped outside the tea-room on Tanjor Road, the mouth of the Mlazi ahead of them. Cray lifted his face to the moon and forced his breathing under control. He looked over at Forrester.

'Have you spoken to your dad about this?'

'Why?'

'Have you?'

'Ja.'

'And what did he say?'

'He said don't get involved.'

'That's exactly what I'm saying: don't get involved, Jack.'

'I can't help it. Thanks to Jackson I'm already involved. I need to know what's going on.'

'No, you don't. Take it for granted that the CIS is right and that Baston's murder has nothing to do with organised crime or politics. Just solve the case. Solve it, and forget about it. That's my advice.'

'I can't do that.'

'I'm afraid that's probably something you will live to regret.'

'I don't care, Chris. I want to know what's really going on. I'm pissed off that they've given me a murder to investigate and won't even tell me the real identity of the body, never mind details about him. I'm pissed off, and I want to know.'

'Are you sure?'

'Ja.'

'Okay, let's head back, and I'll tell you what I know.'

They began the run north, and as soon

as they found their pace again, Cray began. 'What I know about this is complicated; that you must understand. Also, that I don't know the truth about everything. I can only guess at the bits I don't know. Which brings me to my unit, the CIS. How many of us do you think there are at the Aliwal Street offices?'

'What, you mean your total strength? I don't know, I never thought about it.'

'Twenty-one.'

'Is that all?'

'*Ja*, just twenty-one of us. There've been severe cutbacks since the elections — which has resulted in the budget for external security being drastically reduced.'

'By external security you mean operations abroad?'

'*Ja*.'

'So the CIS does operate overseas?'

'*Ja*, but much less so than it used to. There's only twenty-one of us at Boland and we're by far the biggest office in KwaZulu-Natal. So it's a close-knit, secretive, and shrinking organisation we're talking about. You know my two colleagues and what work we do. Richard and I present what you might call the public face of the CIS in Durban. It's no secret what we do, and it's believed that our role is primarily a liaison one.

'The point I'm making in telling you this is that the CIS keeps its internal and external functioning entirely separate, or at least every effort is made to do so. I am, very obviously, part of the internal security function. As such I therefore know little about external operations. Even more than that, because of our public function, Richard and I are to a certain extent removed from the other internal functions as well.'

'You mean you never work on anything else?'

'*Ja*, not unless it's directly related to our liaison jobs. It has its good points and bad, but every day I go to work I do almost exactly the same job. Andre is the only one who ever gets used for anything else. So, in a way, because of his photography, Andre probably knows more about the rest of our unit than either Richard or I do, despite the fact that we outrank him. I'm telling you this so you don't think I'm keeping anything from you or being mysterious, okay?'

'I don't think you are.'

'Good, then don't ask any more questions because it's story-time . . . '

Cray's story started off much the same as Jackson's had. It began with organised crime in Durban; criminals with links to gangs from China and perhaps Cape Town; criminals importing heroin from the Middle and Far East to supply the relatively new demand in South Africa. It was a growth industry. Most of what Jackson had told Forrester in that regard was true, according to Cray, including the involvement of the CIS being due to Mannikum's link with APLA.

When the veneer of organised crime was removed, however, PAGAD was revealed lurking beneath. The founder members, Jaffer and Edries, had very recently lost control of the organisation — lost it to an Islamic fundamentalist named Abdus Salaam Ebrahim. Ebrahim was a radical who actively promoted violence. He was believed, with his associate Fazil Mohammed Domingo, to have been responsible for the murder of Rashaad Staggie and the attacks on the police at the demonstration in Cape Town. He now styled himself PAGAD's National Coordinator. While Faroek Jaffer had willingly stood down from his position as leader, Nadthmi Edries had resisted Ebrahim's takeover.

Right up until he went missing.

Ebrahim's leadership, it was believed, heralded a new, more dangerous stage in PAGAD's development, and the CIS were watching closely. Michael David, as Durban's regional coordinator, actually held very little sway in PAGAD. Ephraim El-Essani was the Provincial Coordinator in KwaZulu-Natal, but as PAGAD's only branch was in Durban, David's title was nominal only, and he was really just El-Essani's deputy.

The CIS were watching a power struggle unfold between El-Essani and David, and El-Essani was currently trying to discredit David in the Durban mosques. El-Essani was believed to be heavily-reliant upon Domingo, on loan from Ebrahim. Cray surmised that

David's involvement in the heroin trade might have caused embarrassment to PAGAD, given that they were officially militantly anti-drug. David, like Mannikum, had also been a member of APLA. Unlike Mannikum, there was no record of him ever having left the organisation.

Forrester was surprised at that, and interrupted. 'I've been wondering about David, there's something that didn't make much sense to me.'

'What's that?'

'The arms. He's gun-running to North Africa and Europe, but why bother? Why bother when you're sitting on a fortune in heroin with contracts from the Triads and, ounce for ounce, making miles more money with the drugs than you ever will with the guns? And the drugs are so much easier to move.'

Cray didn't answer at first, then asked, 'When did you join?'

'January, 1992.'

'Do you remember the bomb that exploded on a Mynah bus in town in December 1993?'

'*Ja*, the bus was at Smith and Gardiner.

There was a bank robber in the back, planning a hold-up with a hand grenade. He was fiddling about with it and it exploded, killing him and a couple of others. That the one?'

'*Ja*, but Welcome Nxumahlo was no bank robber. He was a member of APLA. He was supposed to be attacking a police station that night, but he cocked up. Do you remember what happened in Pine Street the next month, January 1994?'

'The attack on the police sub-station?'

'*Ja*. A student from ML Sultan Technikon named Mohseen Jeenah led two APLA men in an attack on the police reporting office at the Pine Street Parkade. But we had a tip-off, and instead of two lazy specials dozing in the charge office, the Task Force was waiting. Jeenah lobbed in his grenade, pointed his AK47, and all hell broke loose. He and one of his men were killed, the other badly wounded. It was the last terrorist attack before the elections; the last official terrorist attack in South Africa, in fact.'

'I can't remember, was Jeenah acting on his own, or did he have the sanction of APLA?'

'He had their sanction. Remember, despite Mandela's orders to down tools in 1990, APLA continued attacking farmers and policemen right up to the elections. You can see why the ANC were pissed off: APLA was busy destabilising the very process that was certain to give Mandela the presidency.'

'How does this relate to David and PAGAD?'

'Patience. Don't interrupt.'

'Sorry.'

'The APLA commander of the Durban cell, the man responsible for Nxumahlo and Jeenah, was Abdul Daoud Raoof. After Jeenah's botched attack — especially as it had left one of his men alive and in CIS hands — Raoof knew his days were numbered. Six weeks later the CIS came for him and another APLA member, a colleague of Nxumahlo. They caught his crony, but Raoof escaped to Paarl.

'There were three main APLA cells

operating in South Africa: one in Jo'burg, one in Durban, and one in Paarl, with a Cape Town sub-cell. I joined the CIS in April that year, and Raoof was top priority. He'd escaped again in Paarl, and it was believed he was hiding in Jo'burg at the time. The National Intelligence Agency were also involved in tracking him down and Raoof was forced to flee the country, via Botswana I believe. The next I heard of him was in November of that year, when he was in *Dar es Salaam*, in Tanzania.'

'Wasn't that where APLA had their headquarters?'

'That's right. It's been APLA's external headquarters since 1964. I'm not sure exactly what went on in *Dar es Salaam*, all I know is that Raoof became involved with one of the many Islamic fundamentalist groups out there and went to America early in 1995. Someone else in my story was also in America that year: Domingo, Ephraim El-Essani's right-hand man in Durban.

'Domingo, originally from Malaysia, was educated in Cape Town, and visited both *Dar es Salaam* and New York in 1995. At the end of 1995, Raoof and a guy called Wadih el Hage were under surveillance by the FBI in Texas. It was believed that Domingo was connected to one or both of them. In November 1995 I was commissioned and joined Richard where I am now, so I lost track of what happened. All I know for certain was that Domingo returned to Cape Town at the beginning of last year and became — along with Ebrahim — one of the first members of PAGAD.'

'So PAGAD is connected to APLA.'

'Yes, but that's not particularly important. The connection goes beyond PAGAD and APLA to Moslem fundamentalism and international terrorism. Raoof, a Moslem APLA commander, joined el Hage. El Hage is a Kenyan national and is believed to be connected to a network of Islamic fundamentalists run from Saudi Arabia and with bases in Afghanistan and the Sudan . . . '

'Called?'

'I'm not sure if anybody knows that at the moment. *I* certainly don't. But this group are supposed to be powerful, with hundreds of members worldwide, possibly even a thousand. They've been linked to the guerrilla assault on American troops in Mogadishu in 1993, and two attacks on Americans in Saudi Arabia — in 1995 and last year. I believe that el Hage is in the frame for his involvement in the bombings.'

'And Raoof?'

'I don't know. More relevant to you is the fact that Jeenah and Michael David were members of the same APLA cell in Durban. And I think it's safe to assume that David at least knew Raoof, if not being an actual associate.'

'So David is connected not only to PAGAD, but to this other international Moslem organisation as well?'

'It seems like it. You can answer your own question about the arms now, can't you?'

Forrester strained his brow in concentration, 'David's working for PAGAD and or this other organisation to move the guns for his Moslem brothers, isn't he? The heroin, the drugs, and the Triads

— they're just about funding the guns, aren't they?'

'*Ja*, that's what the CIS suspects. David has criminal connections worldwide, connections that seem to be centred around the arms, rather than the drugs. The fact that he appears to be behind the murder of van Niekerk and Baston is also suggestive, when you consider that a British Moslem carried it out. Do you know anything about this man, Zaoui?'

'No, Jackson gave me nothing, and there's next to nothing in the papers. Just that he was Moslem and a British citizen.'

'I don't know anymore myself, unfortunately. But I know that David's connected to an international Moslem terror organisation, and gun-running to his colleagues in Britain. So when a British Moslem shows up and kills the two men after David, well, it's not exactly rocket science to put him in the frame.'

'So you're telling me that Robert Baston, van Niekerk and Michael Baston were all killed by David, PAGAD, or some other — faceless — Moslem extremists?'

'No, I'm not. I'm telling you that Inspector Jackson, as well as making up his own stories, is really telling you that the CIS doesn't think that Superintendent Baston was killed by any of the groups you mentioned. Unlike his brother and the captain.'

'And he's telling me the truth?'

'He's telling you what he thinks is the truth.'

'And what the CIS thinks is the truth?'

'Don't ask me that. I've already told you I don't know.'

'Sorry, I know.'

'Incidentally, there are also still CIS men after the mastermind behind the 1994 Pine Street attack.'

'You're kidding! Three years later?'

'*Ja.*'

'Who is it?'

'If I did know, I wouldn't tell you,' Cray gave a taciturn smile.

'Shit, where does all this leave me?'

'Right back to what I said at the beginning: solve the murder and forget about everything, especially everything you've heard from me tonight.'

'One last question, then I promise to shut up and go away.' They had passed Treasure Beach and could see the lights of Brighton Beach in the distance up ahead.

'*Ja*?'

'What can you tell me about Robert Baston?'

'You mean Birch Baston?'

'Who? Oh, *ja*, I saw that in the papers.'

'Everybody called him Birch.'

'Why?'

'No idea.'

'How well did you know him, did he ever mention having a brother?'

'He joined us just after I'd started work with Richard, so — although he was internal security — we never worked together. I never knew anything about him other than that he spent a lot of time travelling around the province. We spoke briefly once or twice, but that was it. I can tell you two things for definite only.'

'What?'

'He lived in Bellair, but he spent a lot of time in Durban North.'

'In Durban North?'

'*Ja.*'

'What, working?'

Cray ignored the question, 'He was there when Sergeant de Gouveia was shot.'

'At the butchers in Maryland?'

'*Ja*, and that's all you're going to get from me, Superintendent.'

'What's the second thing?'

'Bellair: first thing; Durban North: second thing.'

Forrester could see he wasn't going to get any more out of Cray and they finished the run as they had begun, in silence.

He tried to put his thoughts in some kind of order on his way home. Cray had, as predicted, given him a wealth of information. Too much, even. What practical effect did APLA, PAGAD, Triads, and Moslem terrorists have on Forrester's case? Nothing, if someone else had killed him. Everything, if the CIS were wrong about it not being work-related. Suddenly it wasn't just David who might want him dead, but at least two powerful organisations, three if you threw in the Triads.

The CIS had to be wrong.

David was a powerful man in his own right and he'd everything to lose when Michael Baston came knocking at his door. Was he likely to just flee without exacting any revenge? Forrester didn't think so.

No way.

The closer he got to home, the more certain Forrester became that the CIS had overlooked something in their investigation. There were so many links — PAGAD, APLA, el Hage — they must have missed something.

Forrester would just have to continue the charade until he could find out more about David's connections.

# 7

## The Grey Street Mosque

Jackson was talking on the phone when Forrester walked into their office at five to eight on Wednesday morning. Forrester's plan was to extend their search of establishments likely to be frequented by Baston to Umhlanga, and perhaps even Westville if necessary, in order to build a more complete picture of his life. He was also contemplating a return visit to Angela — but on his own.

Jackson ended his call, coughed, cleared his throat, and addressed Forrester, 'Morning, Superintendent, I've got some news for you.'

'*Ja?*'

'Angela Broad's alibi has been confirmed by her friend, but I couldn't find anything for Dave Rich. Did you contact his brother?'

'*Ja*, he left a message for me last night.

95

I'll try him again this evening.'

'Also, I've got us a name for the brunette.'

'And how did you do that?'

'Well, I just tried his two buddies, Menye and van der Westhuizen — did they perhaps escape your mind?'

'And?' Forrester's stare was cold, his tone cutting.

'Just Penelope. It's not a lot, but it's a start.'

It was a start; more than likely the start of false trail.

Forrester doubted they'd get anywhere until they were able to interview Andrews and the elder Rich, but Andrews wasn't due back for ten days and Rich was proving difficult to get hold of. He didn't mention it to Jackson because he wanted to make sure he saw both men on his own. 'Then I think it's time we woke up the manager of The Langoustine,' he said. He found the man's number and dialled.

Jackson cleared his throat again, and took a swig of his Coke. Forrester wondered again if he was a smoker, or if he was coming down with 'flu'.

Harvey wasn't too pleased to receive Forrester's call that early in the first place; he was even less pleased when he discovered what he wanted. But there wasn't a lot he could do about it, so he found himself opening up the restaurant at nine o'clock, under the watchful eyes of the two policemen. He found the one with the horrible scar particularly unnerving.

An hour later, Forrester and Jackson had the names, addresses, and telephone numbers of all eleven current members of staff who'd been working at the restaurant in October 1995. Much to Harvey's chagrin, Forrester, now seated at the bar, showed no signs of leaving, and asked for two cups of coffee. With a sigh of annoyance, he sloped off to the kitchen to fetch fresh milk.

Forrester started at the top of the list and Jackson at the bottom. Forty-five minutes and two cups of coffee later, they had reached four of the eleven people. All four were women, and three still lived in Durban North. Forrester had made sure that they took both cars to the restaurant, both for practical reasons and because he, once again, had his own agenda to pursue. It would have made sense for Forrester to do the Durban North interviews himself — he might know the girls or perhaps family members — but he left them to Jackson and took the one in Westville himself.

In Dawncliffe he spoke to a plain young woman by the name of Lenore. Despite her enthusiasm she was unable to give him any information on Baston or Penelope. Forrester was on his way back to town, speeding down the Western Freeway, when Jackson called. Penelope Hunter. No address or personal information except that she'd matriculated at Northlands Girls High School and played tennis for the South African Schools team in 1991. Jackson seemed quite pleased with himself, however, and Forrester agreed to meet him back in the office, by which time Jackson hoped to have an address to go with the name.

Northlands Girls High class of 1991? That would have put her one year above Rose. They might have known one another; certainly Rose would have known of Penelope Hunter. Forrester wondered if she might have met one of the Bastons, until he started wondering which one, and confused himself.

His thoughts soon returned to what Cray had told him the previous night. APLA, PAGAD, el Hage, Moslem fundamentalists, international terrorism . . . but while Forrester was intrigued by the mystery of Baston's death, he was — perversely — even more interested in whether there had actually been one or two murders.

Were the Bastons one or two people?

Cray obviously didn't know, but he'd made it clear that Forrester's idea of the two identities for a single man wasn't far fetched. There was little point in checking police records, records of either of the identities, Robert Baston's murder, Zaoui's arrest, or even the murder of Mr and Mrs Baston in Knysna; Forrester had no doubt that all of the necessary information would be faked. The only way to find out conclusively was to go to the Cape himself and find out first hand whether there were one or two brothers.

But he didn't have the time for that.

He resented being away from his unit as it was, without wasting even more time by crossing the breadth of the country just to satisfy his curiosity. There were more important things he should be doing, like ferreting out the bad apples from the former Ntuzuma Detective Branch and the Met Dog Unit. So who the hell cared whether the dead superintendent was really Michael or Birch Baston, or if Jackson was telling the truth? It didn't matter. All that mattered was finding the damn suspect so that Forrester could get back to work.

There was something else Cray had said, something that didn't seem to involve politics or terrorists. What was Robert Baston doing spending time in Durban North? There had definitely been a hint there about something. But what? Cray would have told him if he'd known that the two brothers were one and the same.

Wouldn't he?

Sergeant de Gouveia had belonged to

the Internal Stability Unit's RDP Assist Unit, a plainclothes group set up specifically to combat the theft and robbery of the materials the government was pouring into the previously deprived areas. The unit was known to be hardworking and successful — and to have a high casualty rate.

De Gouveia was off-duty, shopping at the small Maryland Centre last March, when an armed robbery had taken place at the butchers he was in. He had attempted to draw his firearm, but the two suspects were too quick, and shot him in the head before aborting the robbery and making their escape. It had been a gutsy, if futile attempt. And Robert Baston was there? Forrester would have to find out about that. All he knew was that Murder and Robbery had shot both suspects dead five week's later. Nothing about any CIS involvement. It was just another anomaly in a case which was complicated enough already.

Forrester checked his watch as he entered the city centre: it was just after eleven-fifteen . . . the timing was perfect.

There were three mosques in Durban: Grey Street in the town centre, Randles Road in Sydenham, and Soofie Sahet in Durban North. The Grey Street one was not only the oldest and largest, but also — of more interest to Forrester — the workplace of an *imam* by the name of Devnerain. Mr Devnerain's son, Sergeant Jack Devnerain, had died while under Forrester's command on a dusty afternoon in Ntuzuma two year's ago.

Jack, like Forrester, had been a university graduate, but had decided to join the SAPS as a constable as opposed to an officer candidate. He'd wanted to work his way up from the bottom, taking each step only when he felt that he'd learned enough to deal with the increased responsibility. It was typical of his single-minded, dedicated approach to his work. He was also a devout Moslem, and his father had been proud of both his devotion to his faith, as well as his service to his community and country.

Forrester and Jack were both volunteers for Unit 9 of the Internal Stability Unit, considered one of the most dangerous jobs for a policeman in Durban. Jack was already there when Forrester joined, and the two men took an instant liking to one another. They had become firm friends, the difference in rank never a problem. It was Forrester who went to break the news of Jack's death to his father. The man was devastated, but stoical: it had been God's will. Forrester had visited Mr Devnerain from time to time in the intervening years, sometimes at his home in Sparks, and sometimes at the mosque.

He was just the man to ask about PAGAD and David.

Forrester parked illegally in Cathedral Street, and jostled his way through the crowded pavements to the mosque. He left his shoes in the antechamber, and took the stairs up to Devnerain's office. The *imam* was in, as Forrester had suspected; he usually led *Dhuhr*, the midday prayer.

'*Salaam aleikum.*'

'*Wa aleikum as-salaam.*' The *imam* embraced him.

Forrester closed the door and sat

opposite him. 'I'm afraid it's business today, Mr Devnerain.'

'Oh yes, do the police service require my help?'

'This policeman does.'

'Of course, my son, how may I help?'

'What can you tell me about PAGAD — in Durban, that is?'

'Pah!' The old man spat, muttered a curse in Arabic, and spoke calmly to Jack. 'That was wrong of me, my son. None of us holds the key to Allah's will, but sometimes I forget my humility by thinking that a minority of our brothers are easily led astray by false prophets. PAGAD is run from Randles Road, and although I have prayed with members — as have my brothers in Durban North — we do not support the organisation.'

'Why not?'

'To begin with, PAGAD was formed last year in the Cape Flats as a totally secular group. It was a gathering of citizens, victims of local villains, who wanted to defend themselves from drugs and crime. A group with . . . with noble ideals.

'But this very quickly seems to have become a paramilitary movement, and has turned into some kind of misguided *jihad*. No, I have never supported it and this year, when they shot at policemen from behind their women, my suspicions were confirmed. No doubt there are many good brothers in their ranks, but I do not — I will not — promote such a vigilante group.'

'I quite understand. Can you tell me anything about Michael David?'

'May Allah forgive me for my pride, but the man is a disgrace to the faith. He is no more Moslem than the whores on Point Road. I wasn't surprised when I read of his downfall, no doubt he has run to join the other unclean in Cape Town. Good riddance, I said, good riddance to bad rubbish.'

'Strictly between you and I, Mr Devnerain, Michael David has been responsible for the death of at least two policemen. What I'm wondering is if he still has enough influence to have had a third policeman killed after he went on the run. Do you know anyone who might know that kind of information and who might be willing to talk to me?'

Devnerain paused before he answered, 'I know a man in Sydenham who will talk to you. How much he knows, I cannot say. What I can tell you though, my son, is that this David is a powerful and evil man. You know about Domingo?'

'Fazil Mohammed Domingo?'

'Yes, that is the man. Domingo is the right hand of Abdus Salaam Ebrahim. Ebrahim has just taken the leadership of PAGAD from Jaffer and Edries. When he proclaimed himself like a false prophet, the national leader Jaffer made way for him, but Edries did not. I have heard from my brothers in Cape Town that Ebrahim has killed him and burned his body, just like he did to that gang leader rubbish last year.'

'Ebrahim did that?'

'It is common knowledge, but no one will go to the police. Where Domingo is, so is Ebrahim. So if you think David had a reason to kill this unfortunate police-man, I would look to Ebrahim's PAGAD to find my culprit.'

'But I heard there was a power struggle between the two, that El-Essani had distanced himself from David and that he and Domingo really ran the organisation.'

'That may be the case, but remember also that Ebrahim and Domingo have themselves to protect. They have themselves to protect and an organisation of misguided fanatics at their service. My son, it is time for me to wash. Here, let me give you the address of my brother in Sydenham. His name is . . . '

Jack took the piece of paper Devnerain handed him, then thanked him. '*Salaam*, my father.'

'*Salaam*, my son.'

They embraced again, and Forrester left. He heard the call to the faithful begin as he climbed in his car.

# 8

## Two Arrests

Jackson was having difficulty locating Penelope Hunter.

Forrester phoned up Northlands Girls High and acquired what details he could. When she'd matriculated in 1991, her address had been James Place, in Virginia, Durban North. Forrester calculated that she would have been twenty-two at the oldest, in 1995. Twelve years younger than Michael Baston. Angela was also younger than him. Perhaps he'd preferred his women that way. It might make them less likely to ask questions and less likely to want to settle down with him — both of which might be problems if he was running two identities. Penelope had lived with her mother and a younger brother, her parents being divorced; her mother's name was Wendy. Forrester couldn't find anything for Wendy Hunter, but then reflected that she might have reverted to her maiden name or remarried.

Jackson was still hard at work on Miss Hunter's whereabouts, and Forrester thought about going to Sydenham to speak to Mr Devnerain's friend. It seemed much more relevant to finding Baston's killer than tracking down some casual fling — or whatever she turned out to be — the man had had two year's ago. He tried Steve Rich again, without success, and was just concocting a story to cover his trip to Sydenham when, on a whim, he changed his mind and settled on a visit to James Place instead.

He told Jackson his destination, and set off north again. He didn't expect to find Wendy Hunter, or any Wendy for that matter, still at James Place, but he was hoping for a forwarding address. He got the address from the current occupant, a very good-looking middle-aged woman called Jackie. He declined her offer of a drink — tea, or perhaps something stronger — and drove up to Umhlanga Rocks Drive, heading for Tipuana Road. As he passed Maryland Centre, he slowed and pulled in to a parking space. Traffic was getting busy and cars were already queuing in Maryland, at the T-junction with Umhlanga Rocks Drive.

Forrester crossed the road and found Booker's Butchery next to a bottle-store advertising discounted liquor. There were about five people at the counter, with two behind cutting, weighing, and packaging. Forrester approached the elder of the employees, who turned out to be the owner, and showed his ID. Craig Booker was happy to help, and after his wife had replaced him at the counter, he showed Forrester to a quieter room at the back.

Booker himself had been in the shop when it was robbed. He was eternally grateful for Sergeant de Gouveia's sacrifice and had no doubt that the men had intended to kill him and his wife once they'd completed the robbery. He recognised the photo of Robert Baston. He'd been the first policeman to respond to the gunfire. How long? He'd been there a minute later, no more. He'd set off after the robbers, following them up Lydia Road. Booker didn't know if he'd seen or engaged them, only that he'd returned to the shop shortly after giving chase — by which time de Gouveia was already dead. Had Baston arrived in a car? No, he'd arrived on foot — from nowhere, it seemed. Booker hadn't seen Baston either before or since the robbery.

Forrester thanked him for his help, and walked back outside.

He was just about to cross the road back to his car when he heard a police radio broadcast over a loudspeaker. Startled, he looked around to his right and saw a Metropolitan Police motorbike parked between Lydia Road and Umhlanga Rocks Drive. It was the patrolman about to take up his rush hour point duty, directing traffic at the T-junction. Forrester hesitated for a second, then approached the man, PC 266 according to his badge.

'Afternoon, constable, I'm Senior Superintendent Forrester, from the Square.'

The man straightened, and offered a quick salute, 'Afternoon, sir.'

'Is this your regular point?'

'Pretty much. I usually manage to pick

it up for either the morning or afternoon stint.'

'How long have you been working here?'

'I've been on motor patrol for three years, been working out of Phoenix for nearly two. Why, sir?'

'Were you here last year when the SAPS sergeant was shot?'

'*Ja*, not at the time. He was shot after I'd already left the point, of course — I was on the morning shift. I responded, but we didn't get anyone.'

'No, I know.'

'Do you recognise this man?' He showed the photo of Robert Baston.

'*Ja*, I do. He's a detective, I think. He was in the butchers, with the sergeant, when I got here.'

'Do you know his name?'

'I don't know him, as such, sir, but I see him around all the time.'

'You do? Where?'

'Here,' he pointed over the road to a large house set well back from Umhlanga Rocks Drive, grinning.

'Here? I'm confused, Constable.'

112

'*Ja*. He's a regular visitor to number eighty-nine. There's a very hot mommy that comes out of there most mornings. Drives a big, white Mercedes; long blonde hair, pink lipstick, tanned . . . nice. She likes the cops too; always thanks me when I let her out of her driveway.'

'And this man was visiting that house — regularly?'

'*Ja*, but only after her husband was gone. I see him first thing every morning, normally while I'm still parking up. He's always gone first thing. Also drives a big, white Merc — nicer model, though. Not too long after, the cop arrives. Sometimes he only stays for half an hour, other times he's still here when I go. That cop's not in the shit is he?'

'No, why?'

'It's just one of our dog handlers told me — he's from Durban North, you know — that her husband's a big shot Lebanese businessman. He hasn't made a complaint has he?'

'No, not yet anyway. When did you last see the detective?'

'Probably last month, sometime. I

haven't seen him for a few weeks, which is unusual. Maybe a bit more than that, actually. I thought he's probably going round later in the day. Or maybe she's been meeting him somewhere.'

Forrester didn't tell the man that the reason for Baston's absence was his death. 'What about this man, have you ever seen him?' He showed the constable the photo of Michael Baston.

He examined it closely. 'Can't say I have, sir, sorry. Looks a bit like the other guy. Is it his brother or something?'

'Something like that. You've been very helpful, Constable, thanks for your time.'

'No problem, sir.'

Forrester went back to his car. So that was why Robert Baston was spending time in Durban North. That was why he'd appeared at the shooting. Forrester remembered something he'd read recently about the involvement of the small, wealthy Lebanese community in illegal activities. Perhaps the husband was connected to organised crime and that was what had caused Baston's death — both deaths? Was Baston having an affair with the woman in both of his guises?

But that didn't explain the assassination of Captain van Niekerk. No, it wasn't worth thinking about at the moment, so he filed it away along with all the other unexplained pieces of information.

He waved at the constable as he turned left onto Umhlanga Rocks Drive, and then made a right, descending into the suburb of Glen Hills.

He'd just found Tipuana Road when Jackson rang.

Penelope Hunter lived in Broadlands, a simplex development in Prospect Hall Road, just across from the Hypermarket-by-the-Sea; she worked as the PA to the managing director of Corobrik, in North Coast Road. Forrester checked his watch, and told Jackson to arrange to meet her at home immediately after work.

Jackson rung off and Forrester found the address he was looking for. It was another duplex development. Simplexes and duplexes seemed to be increasingly popular these days: not only were they cheaper than detached or semi-detached houses, but they offered a greater degree of security. Some employed their own security guards as an additional service to attract prospective buyers.

Forrester parked across the road from the entrance to Greenview, and waited for Jackson to call back. The call came a few minutes later: half-past four at 84 Broadlands. There was something else as well: an hour and a half ago CIS members had shot Michael David dead in Wellington, near Paarl, in an old APLA safe-house. He'd been there with an unidentified accomplice who had been wounded and was now in police custody. Jackson hung up.

Forrester drove back towards the river. David: dead. Had the CIS executed him? Like Murder and Robbery, they often didn't take suspects alive. Especially cop-killers. Cop-killers always died. Those were just the rules, everybody knew it: if you killed a policeman you better make sure they never caught you. So, did that mean that someone in the CIS thought David responsible for Michael Baston's death? Or had David really come out shooting? He was, after all, a trained terrorist. And wouldn't the CIS have wanted him alive. *Ja* . . . unless he'd killed a policeman.

Forrester had been parked outside 84 Broadlands for three minutes when Jackson pulled up next to him at twenty-five past four. Forrester pushed the button to slide his passenger window down.

'She here yet?' Jackson asked.

'Not unless she got home before quarter past.'

Jackson looked in his rear view mirror, 'I think this might be her now.'

Forrester twisted in his seat and saw a young brunette in a smart white Golf. Jackson moved his car to let her past and she parked outside the garage of number 84. Forrester debussed and locked his car, watching the woman as she did the same. Harvey's description had been entirely accurate. She was wearing a baggy summer suit with trousers over a black blouse, and rather large dark glasses. She was very pretty, with high cheekbones, a button nose, full lips, and a dark tan. She wore no make-up. Her suit was too baggy for Forrester to discern her figure, but she was obviously athletic.

As he approached her, Forrester noticed that her fingers were long and the nails had all been chewed. He wondered that she didn't make more of her looks and figure, particularly as a PA. With a little touching up, she would easily make the step from pretty to beautiful. Perhaps that was exactly what she wanted to avoid. She was only twenty-four, yet already held an excellent job; perhaps she didn't want people thinking she'd got it because she was attractive; perhaps she wanted to ensure people took her seriously.

'Hello, ma'am, I'm Jack Forrester. I'm a senior superintendent with the police,' he held out his hand, which she took firmly.

'Hello, superintendent, I'm Penelope Hunter.' Forrester turned to see Jackson approaching. 'This is Inspector Jackson, my colleague.'

'*Howzit,*' Jackson said, taking her hand.

'Come inside, gents,' she said, 'please excuse the mess, I wasn't expecting anyone.' She unlocked the door and led them into the simplex. Simplexes were built in a similar terraced fashion to duplexes, except that they were on a single level.

As he had expected, Forrester was led through a small alcove into an open-plan kitchen and living room. The room was large and spacious, however, and there were French doors — protected by a burglar-guard gate — at the rear. Two passages led off and Forrester thought it was probably a two-bedroom home. Despite Penelope's comment, it was immaculate. It was decorated in an artistic, minimalist style with Italian tiles and pastel colours. The items of furniture were obviously carefully selected and expensive. 'Sit down,' she said, waving them to the couch; 'I'll be with you in a minute.'

She disappeared off to the left. Jackson took a seat, but Forrester strolled casually over to the far wall to have a look at one of the prints.

He was just a little ill at ease.

It was probably nothing, but he didn't like the fact that Penelope had disappeared from sight as soon as she'd entered the house. He was probably just being over-cautious: nothing suspicious at all. Except . . . well, the only thing was that when Forrester had looked at the crime scene photographs, a thought had immediately popped into his head. He knew this case had given his imagination a little too much reign, but he'd thought that Michael Baston was dressed like he was expecting female company.

How, exactly, was that?

Forrester couldn't even answer his own question. It was just an idea, no doubt a misguided intuition, but that was the impression he'd received. So perhaps this wasn't a waste of time. Perhaps Penelope Hunter had been involved with Michael Baston right up to his demise. Perhaps she knew something that would put them on the right track.

Without realising it, Forrester had wandered off into the kitchen. Like the living area, it was neat and minimalist. So clean that it looked unused; brand new, like a show house. He looked over to Jackson, sitting on the couch, and saw a set of kitchen knives in their wooden holder. He moved to join Jackson when he suddenly turned back to the kitchen.

He noticed three things simultaneously: the knives were branded 'Wilkinson', there was one missing, and there was no dishwasher.

'Thank you, gentlemen, now, what can I . . . ' Penelope had walked back into the room.

'Jackson!'

The inspector jumped to his feet, not sure why but hearing the urgency in Forrester's voice. Both men faced the woman. She'd taken off her jacket to reveal taught, tanned arms. She held Forrester's gaze for ten full seconds, betraying nothing. Then she glanced over to the kitchen, down at the floor, and her face reddened. When she looked up at Forrester again, there was defiance in her eyes.

'Fuck you,' she said.

Forrester took her arm. 'I'm arresting you for the murder of Michael Baston. You do not have to answer this charge until you have a lawyer present, but I must warn you that anything you say will be recorded and may be used as evidence against you . . . '

# 9

## Birch Baston

Penelope Hunter, in the presence of her lawyer, had made a full confession on Wednesday night. Michael Baston had contacted her on the weekend and arranged for her to come and visit him on the Monday night. She had done so, taking the kitchen knife with her and stabbing him to death. After she'd killed him she'd panicked, taking the crowbar from his boot and faking a break-in. Too late, she realised she'd faked a break-out, and made a half-hearted attempt to cover it up before leaving with Baston's watch, wallet, and firearms. She'd dumped them all in a skip on the way home.

Why had she killed him? Because he hadn't kept in touch with her as he had promised when he left for America. Go figure. The woman was clearly unhinged, but Forrester had solved the case in three days after the CIS had got nowhere in seven. Everyone was impressed, even the CIS.

Thursday had been an emotional day for Forrester. He'd returned to the Special Investigations Unit office to the cheers of the four men present: handshakes and congratulations all round. Not only were they pleased at his success, but they were happy to have him back because it meant the director was returning upstairs. Subramanny was next, but he also had bad news for Forrester: in his three days running the Special Investigations Unit, he'd uncovered something untoward. He would say no more, but District Commissioner Smit would be seeing Forrester about it later.

Detective Superintendent Gadesh Sukunan, Forrester's deputy, briefed him prior to the meeting. The video evidence of the Met police dog handlers had gone missing. The Field Unit had sole possession of the tape as they were working the case on their own. It did not look good: either it was gross incompetence, or — even worse — corruption. Either way it was Forrester's responsibility. He was expecting the worst when he got the phone call from Smit.

But the District Commissioner congratulated him on his outstanding success with the CIS and lavished him with smiles and praise. When he raised the subject of the video tape, he didn't even give Forrester the opportunity to take responsibility; it was almost as if it didn't matter because the Special Investigations Unit was being closed down the next month anyway.

Forrester couldn't believe it. He wondered how long Smit had known.

There were more smiles from the District Commissioner. The Special Investigations Unit was becoming the Special Investigative Unit. This would be a team of investigators run by a senior judge who had been appointed by the state president to oversee anti-corruption investigations. The unit would be staffed by policemen as well as civilians appointed by the judge. It would operate from either Johannesburg or Cape Town. Forrester's own detectives would be absorbed into the Anti-Corruption Unit.

And the Field Unit?

Well, that depended on the result of the Anti-Corruption Unit's internal investigation, but they were both going to be suspended in the mean time.

And Forrester?

Smit's grin was almost obsequious. Forrester was to be offered command of the new unit, a command which would make him a director. He would be the youngest director in the SAPS and Smit had no doubt that the post would give him access to a high-ranking position in the government very soon, if that was what Forrester wanted. It was his personal recommendation, Smit said, and he had no doubt that Forrester was once again the right man for the job. Everything they had discussed today was confidential. The Provincial Commissioner was visiting the Square tomorrow, and he would be making the offer to Forrester formally. More handshakes and congratulations and the meeting was over.

Forrester didn't know what to think. He was relieved that he seemed to be off the hook as far as his Field Unit went. He was also shocked that the unit was disbanding so quickly. He realised that the timing was fortuitous for him, but he still couldn't get over the rapidity with which it was happening. He had had absolutely no idea. Nor could he tell the men yet.

A directorship.

It was unbelievable. Every time he thought he'd made an oversight or a mistake in his career, fortune had smiled on him. This would be his fourth promotion in five and a half years. With two medals for bravery already in his pocket. It was more than he had ever hoped for, and it was quicker than he could have imagined. His father and mother would be so proud. Where would they end up, Johannesburg or Cape Town? He would discuss it with Dee when he got home.

But it was Delia that had the important news on Thursday night: she was pregnant. She had suspected it for a few weeks, but had only had it confirmed that day. One month pregnant. The child was due next February, the month of

Forrester's own birthday.

Suddenly, he had a lot to think about.

He'd always thought that he and Dee would have emigrated by the time they decided to have children. Her pregnancy hadn't been planned this early. Not that Forrester was disappointed, not at all, he just hadn't seriously thought about being a father yet. He didn't want his child growing up in the crime-ridden society they inhabited. That was why he'd planned to emigrate, perhaps to Australia, perhaps to England.

And now it was time to go.

And yet Delia's pregnancy hadn't convinced him of the need to leave. He'd always thought it would. But he was reluctant. Very reluctant. Especially when he'd just found out that next month he could be the youngest director in the country, would be leading a judicial investigation team, and had a future in the government if he played his cards right.

This was a big step for Forrester. Had the Minister of Safety and Security himself chosen him for the job? It seemed possible — no, likely, even. Mr Mafamadi had no doubt earmarked him. Opportunities like this didn't come twice. What did Australia hold for him, or England? Did he really want to leave the police for the private sector to be . . . what, a glorified bookkeeper? Forrester had never been so torn.

And Delia hadn't helped. It was her opinion that they should both come to their own decisions independently, and then discuss it on the weekend. He supposed it made sense, but he'd had no idea how he was going to stall Provincial Commissioner Ngidi on Friday.

The day passed quickly, with leads on the Ntuzuma case taking priority over Forrester's personal problems. It seemed like only the second time he'd checked his watch when it was already ten to five. At last. He hadn't yet decided exactly what he was going to tell Ngidi; he'd wing it when he got there. He was just glad that the waiting was over.

Five minutes later, he got up from his desk and put on his jacket. He checked his appearance in the basin mirror and left the empty office. He walked up the two flights of stairs to the top floor of the police building. It was dark as most of the lights were switched off and the sun was setting outside.

The whole floor seemed deserted.

He made his way past Smit's office — which looked empty — to the smaller one adjacent to it reserved for the Provincial Commissioner when he visited the Square. There was a light on inside. He took a deep breath, gave two sharp raps, and entered.

'Take a seat,' said Jackson, easing his feet off the table.

'What the hell are you doing here!' demanded Forrester.

'I've come to repay you for the help you gave me.'

'Where's the Commissioner?'

'You didn't really expect to see him at five o'clock on a Friday afternoon, did you?'

Forrester had to bite down a retort. He was fuming at having spent the whole day worrying about this meeting only to be met by the flippancy of the CIS inspector.

'I do not find this amusing, Inspector,' he said.

'I'm not here to entertain you.'

'You are wasting my time. But then you've spent most of the bloody week doing that, haven't you?' Jack's voice became louder and he didn't give Jackson time to answer, 'While you've been playing at being a spy, I've been taken off two important cases at an absolutely crucial time. I have no idea what the point of the whole exercise was, but I do not appreciate being led on a wild goose chase by a non-commissioned officer, CIS or not!'

'Are you . . . '

'No, I'm not damn well finished — so listen! I don't know what kind of idiot you take me for, but how the hell you expected me to solve the murder of a man — whoever in God's name he really was — who has multiple identities, I have no idea. I don't give a shit about any of it. That we managed it was a combination of luck and the fact that the suspect is obviously a complete bloody lunatic! Now, I'm not going to tell anyone about this, or be a security risk in any way, and I don't expect to see you ever again. That's all!' He turned and stormed towards the door.

'I'm Birch Baston.'

Forrester stopped and slowly, very slowly, turned back towards Jackson. 'What did you say?'

'I said, I'm Birch Baston.'

Stunned, Forrester, walked slowly back to the desk. He pulled out one of the chairs and sat down heavily. 'So, so there really were two brothers . . . and we really were investigating the murder of Michael Baston?'

'*Ja.*'

'And Birch Baston wasn't investigating his own murder in the form of Michael Baston, he was investigating Michael Baston in the form of you . . . Jackson?'

'*Ja.*'

'You survived the . . . wait a minute . . . you torched your own house?'

'*Ja.*'

'The police chased you from the scene of the crime, because you killed the Brit. How come, wasn't he worth more to you alive?'

Jackson pointed at his scar, 'It wasn't that easy.'

The scar, the cough.

'Christ, I've been a complete idiot. I knew the fire was too obvious, but I was so focused on the similarities between Birch Baston and Michael Baston that I didn't see . . . you . . . right here in front of me. You've lost weight . . . '

'*Ja.*'

'And grown a goatee. Jesus. So, most of what you told me was true. You lost your brother?'

'*Ja*, I did.'

'I'm sorry to hear that. What about your parents?'

'Safe and sound in Knysna, when I spoke to them yesterday . . . touch wood,' he patted the table.

'I would have found out sooner or later.'

'*Ja*, but it was later because you found Hunter first. I'm not here to discuss the case, Superintendent, I'm repaying a favour.'

'So you said. What favour?'

'You found my brother's murderer; I

owe you for that.'

'Go on.'

'You made a very big mistake.'

'Getting involved with you.'

'No, there was nothing you could do about that. Somehow you found out that the organised crime angle leads to PAGAD. You made a mistake when, while working with me, you decided to visit Devnerain at the mosque.'

'Why?'

'Have you heard the name Fazil Mohammed Domingo?'

'Er, I . . . *ja.*'

'Domingo has connected you with us.'

'What, from Devnerain!'

'No, not from him, but from PAGAD sympathisers at Grey Street.'

'Well, I suppose I'll just have to deal with the situation as it arises. Thanks for the warning . . . '

'Superintendent . . . '

'*Ja,* what?'

'I don't think you quite understand. Domingo is not only connected to Michael David, but also Ebrahim and el Hage. Do these names mean anything to you?'

'I know who they are.'

'Then you also know that they are extremely dangerous men. So far, there's been a chain of command connected with this investigation.'

'What do you mean?'

'I mean that Domingo and his allies have identified Inspector Baston, Captain van Niekerk, and Superintendent Baston as their enemies . . . '

'And?'

'As of Wednesday, that list just got longer: Inspector Baston, Captain van Niekerk, Superintendent Baston, and Senior Superintendent Forrester. Three of the four men on that list are dead, superintendent.'

'But Hunter killed your brother . . . '

'She beat PAGAD and el Hage to it.'

'So what about you? What are you going to do?'

'I have more than one reason to thank you, actually, because now that you've cleared up my brother's case for me, I'm being sent to Cape Town on promotion to continue his work. I'm going after Ebrahim.'

'Captain Jackson?'

'*Ja.*'

'So what should I do?'

'I'm not here to give you advice, just to tell you that you're on PAGAD's list. And maybe not just theirs.'

'Meaning?'

'I can't tell you anymore.'

'Well thanks very much,' Forrester replied sarcastically.

'My pleasure,' Jackson stood up and walked towards the door.

'Hold on, Inspector . . . what's your first name?'

'You know, I haven't decided that yet — I've had too much on my mind lately. But it won't matter to you, because you're never going to see me again: so that is all.' He walked out.

Just Jackson.

Although part of Forrester despised Jackson, or Baston, or whoever the hell he was, the other part realised that he really had done him a favour, even if inadvertently.

Forrester had the discussion with Dee when he got home on Friday night. On

Monday, he turned down Provincial Commissioner Ngidi's offer to head the new unit, and on Friday he handed in his resignation. By August he and Dee were in London, spending his first British summer with Rose in Putney.

# 10

## Fatwah

On the 22$^{nd}$ February 1998 Osama Bin Laden, a Saudi Arabian millionaire, issued a *fatwah* stating that it was the duty of all devout Moslems worldwide to kill American citizens wherever they could find them.

On 7$^{th}$ August the American embassy in *Dar es Salaam* was bombed minutes after a similar explosion outside the embassy in Nairobi. Suspicion initially fell on the Egyptian Islamic Jihad group. Eighteen days later, a group calling themselves Muslims Against Global Oppression claimed responsibility for the bombing of the Planet Hollywood restaurant in Cape Town, allegedly in retaliation for American attacks on a suspected weapons factory in Sudan.

In September American authorities arrested Wadih el Hage, a former personal secretary of Bin Laden, in Arlington, Texas. This arrest, among others, connected Bin Laden's organisation, *al-Qaeda* (literally, *the base*), to the earlier attacks on Americans in Somalia and Saudi Arabia.

In November, Abdullah Daoud Raoof was arrested in New York for his involvement in the 1996 attack in Saudi Arabia. The following month, an unnamed Bin Laden aide, in American custody, confirmed that *al-Qaeda* was in fact leading the Moslem world in organised attacks on American targets worldwide. *Al-Qaeda* had originally been formed in 1988 to launch a *jihad* against the Russians in Afghanistan. When the invaders had left, Bin Laden turned his attention to America, expanding his organisation into a worldwide terror network.

The CIS and National Intelligence Agency intensified their efforts to arrest Ebrahim and Domingo without success. The Planet Hollywood bombing was followed by further bombs, and attacks and assassinations directed at American restaurants and bars, the police, the judiciary, and the homosexual community. PAGAD threw off the veil of Muslims Against Global Oppression and claimed the atrocities as their own.

In September 1999 Faroek Jaffer, one of the founders of PAGAD, was murdered after a speech against the extremist leadership of PAGAD. People began to talk about South Africa erupting into an Algerian-style guerrilla war.

In November Captain Jackson of the SAPS Scorpion Squad arrested a Chinese Triad gangster for Faroek's murder. The connection with the Triads was finally proved.

A month later Jackson arrested Abdus-Salaam Ebrahim and his wife, Zanie, at their home in the Cape Flats. Fazil Mohammed Domingo was arrested along with another suspect at a house in Rylands. All were charged with the murder of Rashaad Staggie. The trial was prioritised, but when it finished in May 2000, Ebrahim and his wife were acquitted.

Domingo was found to be a former

member of *al-Qaeda*, but the National Intelligence Agency and Secret Service failed to connect him to the organisation since his return to the country in 1996. Six months after the end of the trial, Captain Jackson resigned from the SAPS.

On 11$^{th}$ September 2001 the whole world became aware, too late, of exactly what *al-Qaeda* were capable of. By that time, PAGAD were believed responsible for a hundred and ten bomb attacks in Cape Town. Hundreds of people had been killed or wounded in the attacks. PAGAD's response to the *al-Qaeda* attacks was to assassinate a judge.

Both organisations remain active to this day.

## THE END

*Other titles in the*
*Linford Mystery Library:*

**THE GARRETT DOSSIER:**
**ALERT STATE BLACK**

**Frederick Nolan**

Charles Garrett, Special Branch's expert in terrorism, is also a victim of its effects: in an aborted assassination attempt, his wife was murdered. Now on a mission to Northern Germany to neutralize a terrorist cell led by the man who murdered his wife, his every move is blocked, and his German undercover ally assassinated. And it gets worse when he discovers a secret project that threatens the future of humanity — for he becomes the one they want to neutralize . . .

# THE BLIND BEAK

## Ernest Dudley

Eighteenth-century London. Blind magistrate Sir John Fielding, 'The Blind Beak', had instigated the Bow Street Runners to combat the hordes of criminals so rife throughout the city. Criminals such as Nick Rathburn, who fights his way out of Newgate Gaol. Then, by a twist of fate, Nick becomes a secret agent for 'The Blind Beak'. However, as Sir John, amid the Gordon Riots, is in the hands of the terrorising mob, Nick faces death on the gallows at Tyburn . . .

# THE SECRET SERVICE

## Rafe McGregor

The CIA want retired Secret Service agent Jackson back on a mission: to foil Operation Condor, a top secret plan conceived by the East German security police in the Cold War, and now in the hands of *al-Qaeda*. But he finds that he is being used as the bait in a trap. His only chance of escape is to discover who passed the plan to *al-Qaeda*. And he suspects that the answer lies in the Caribbean island of Barbados.